DYEING SEASON

A DEWBERRY FARM MYSTERY

KAREN MACINERNEY

GRAY WHALE PRESS

Copyright © 2019 by Karen MacInerney

All rights reserved.

No part of this book may be reproduced in any form or by any electronic or mechanical means, including information storage and retrieval systems, without written permission from the author, except for the use of brief quotations in a book review.

This book is a work of fiction. Names, characters, places, and incidents are either products of the author's imagination or used fictitiously. Any resemblance to actual events or locales or persons, living or dead, is entirely coincidental.

Books in the Dewberry Farm Mystery Series

Killer Jam

Fatal Frost

Deadly Brew

Mistletoe Murder

Dyeing Season

❀ Created with Vellum

1

It was a beautiful morning in Buttercup, Texas. The bluebonnets were carpeting the rolling hills, I had three new kids gallivanting around the pasture, my spring crops were going strong, and the little house I'd spent the last few months renovating was almost ready for habitation.

There were times over the past year or two since quitting my reporting job in Houston and buying my grandmother's farmhouse that I'd questioned my decision. But now, thanks to a few minor windfalls and excellent weather, for the first time, I was feeling optimistic about my prospects. I had three new female kids, my cow had recently calved and was producing tons of milk, and the fields I'd worked so hard to recondition since moving to Buttercup were green with healthy organic vegetables. Plus, it was almost time for Buttercup's first-ever Easter Market, and I had a bunch of new products I was looking forward to selling: egg-shaped soaps in a rainbow of pastel colors, dyed blown eggs, herb starts, and packets of organic egg dye for customers to take home and try themselves.

I was surveying my little kingdom with a feeling of satisfaction when the cell phone buzzed in my pocket. I checked the Caller ID: it was Peter Swenson, a fellow organic farmer. "Have you seen the weather?" he asked when I picked up.

"No," I said, not liking the ominous tone of his voice.

"Hail coming," he said. "Some of it as big as golf balls. Do you have row cover?"

Murphy's Law, I thought to myself. "I do," I said, "but I'm not sure it can handle golf balls. How much time do I have?"

"It'll be here by six," he said. "At least according to the weather." He paused. "Tornadoes, too."

My stomach clenched. "Tornadoes?"

"Maybe," he said. "There's a watch. Just wanted to let you know."

"Thanks," I told him. I stared up at the clear blue sky and sighed, thinking of the saying I'd heard for many years. Don't like the weather in Texas? Wait a few minutes.

"If I get done here," he said, "I'll come over and help."

"Thanks... and thanks for the heads-up," I told him, already jogging toward the barn. "I'm taking care of it right now!"

I'd just finished covering the first row of arugula when I heard somebody roaring down the drive. I looked up to see my friend Quinn's truck, and smiled in relief.

"What are you doing here?" I called to her as she got out of the driver's seat. I was fighting with the breeze that had recently kicked up as I attempted to pin down another sheet of row cover.

"Peter told me what was coming," she announced with a bright smile. She was dressed for the task in overalls, her curly red hair tied up in a green bandanna. Quinn owned the Blue Onion café on the Town Square; I sometimes lent her a hand prepping meals and waiting tables. She had been one of my closest friends since I moved to Buttercup, and had started dating Peter last year. Her previous relationship had been, to put it mildly, less than ideal; it made me happy to see her with such a kind man. "I got an early start on prep work and Katie is handling the lunch shift, so I thought you might need some help," she said.

"I do. You're a lifesaver," I said, picking up a roll of white row cover. "Here... can you grab an end of this while I unroll it?"

"It's like a giant roll of paper towels," she said, grinning.

"I know," I said, grimacing at the long white banner unfurling from the roll. Thankfully, I'd already wrapped the young tomato plants to protect them from chilly nights; I wasn't sure if the clips would hold if we had high winds, but at least they were covered. I looked down at the row cover in my hand, wondering how it would hold up to hail. It didn't look particularly sturdy, but it was all I had. "I don't know if it will be enough, but it's better than nothing."

"What are you going to do with the animals?" Quinn asked, glancing over at the pasture.

"I'll get them into the barn. But I want to get the tender crops covered first," I told her. "And now that I think of it, I'd better get the herb starts inside, just in case; I'm taking them to the Easter Market."

"Speaking of the Easter Market, did you finish your egg dye packets?" she asked. "I saw that you're doing a workshop on natural egg dyeing."

"I finished last week, and I'm ready to go," I said. I'd been looking for ways to expand my business in creative ways: the herb starts and the egg dyes were part of the experiment.

"Good for you! Speaking of eggs, you might want to make sure your chickens are locked down."

"Why?"

"There's a chicken rustler in town," she said.

I stopped what I was doing. "You're kidding me, right?"

"Someone released all of Ed Zapp's chickens last week."

"He just started raising chickens, didn't he?"

Quinn nodded. "Not in the good way, either. They're all crowded into one big room, and they never get any outside time."

"Poor things," I said. I knew factory farming was the way most eggs were produced, but it still troubled me.

"Whoever did it left some spray paint on the side of the house, too."

"Spray paint? Like what?"

"Some kind of letters," she said.

"How about the chickens? Did he find them all?"

"Most of them," she said. "I guess at least they had a little bit of time outside."

"I'm glad I've got my own egg factory," I said, thinking of my small flock. Most of my hens were Rhode Island Reds and Leghorns, but Peter had given me a couple of Araucanas to raise. They hadn't started laying yet, but I was looking forward to collecting blue eggs, and I'd come to enjoy the chickens' spunky personalities. "Speaking of poultry, I imagine Rooster is clueless as to who did it?"

My friend rolled her eyes. "Look up 'clueless' in the dictionary and you'll find a picture of Sheriff Rooster Kocurek."

"Has his wife divorced him yet?" I asked. The two had separated last winter; apparently she got tired of him disappearing to a deer blind with a few cases of Lone Star and his buddies all the time. On the other hand, from what I knew of his personality, if I were married to Rooster, I might view his continued absence as a win.

"Not yet," she said. "She let him move back in, finally, though."

"Poor thing."

"I know. The woman deserves a medal. Or a sainthood."

"Or something," I said. Rooster Kocurek was not only a less-than-ideal husband, at least if Lacey's actions were any indication, but the laziest law enforcement officer I'd ever encountered, and I'd met quite a few in my job as an investigative reporter in Houston. He'd arrested the wrong person at least four times that I could count since I'd moved to Buttercup... which hadn't been that long ago.

"What I want to know is, why hasn't he been fired?" Quinn asked.

"It's a mystery," I said.

"Well, let's not worry about that now," she said as we stretched out another length of row cover. I eyed the sky nervously; a line of dark clouds was approaching from the north, and the goats were starting to get frisky. Something told me the storm might arrive earlier than six. "How's the house renovation coming?"

"Slowly," I said with a groan. "I was hoping I could be ready to rent it out in time for the spring antique fair, but it's not looking good. The workers found some structural issues when we were replacing the floors." With the help of some concerned local citizens, I'd moved a historic house to the farm several months ago; if I hadn't, it likely would have been destroyed, and it had a lot of history... including reports of a ghost. I'd been worried about renovating it, but between a small windfall and some help from the community, I was slowly (very slowly) turning it into a small but adorable living space.

"Did you keep the stenciling in the downstairs?"

"I did," I said. One of the earliest owners had painted a

beautiful blue pattern near the tops of the walls downstairs. I'd repainted many things, including the beaten-up wood floors on the second floor (and now, soon, the floor joists, apparently), but I'd kept the stenciling, cleaning it carefully and wondering about the woman—I don't know how, but I knew it was a woman—who had painted it.

"No more ghostly noises?"

"Nothing unexplainable, anyway. It appears to be ghost-free."

"And your grandmother?" she asked.

Since moving to the farm, I'd often smelled her scent of lavender, and she'd been something of a quiet guiding force. "She's here," I told Quinn. "I can sense her sometimes. It's comforting."

"Maybe she'll help protect your hens," Quinn said. "But I'd recommend putting a padlock on the chicken coop, just in case."

"It seems weird to do that in Buttercup, but you're probably right," I said. I hardly ever locked the house, much less the chicken coop.

"I know it's weird, but it's probably a good idea. Just until they find out who's doing this," she said. "I'd hate for you to lose your hens."

"Me too," I said as we pinned down the last bit of row cover and headed out to round up the livestock.

WE HAD JUST GOTTEN the goats and cows into the barn—the chickens, birdbrains though they might be, had retreated to their coop on their own—when the first rain hit. And it wasn't a gentle shower, either. It was more like steak knives being hurled from the sky.

Quinn and I raced to the farmhouse. I busied myself moving my herb starts indoors, where the rain wouldn't flatten them, while Quinn put a kettle on for tea. The rain pounded on the metal roof as I tucked the last tray of starts into a corner of the living room and headed back to the kitchen. "No hail so far," Quinn said, peering out the window and running a hand through her damp curls. Chuck, my rescue poodle, threw himself at her feet, begging for a snack, or at least a belly rub, as I put a few scones on a plate and ferried them to the table.

"Thanks again for coming to help," I said, looking out at the dark clouds with trepidation. The trees were swaying like crazy as the wind and rain lashed down; I hoped the row cover would hold. "I'm thankful for the rain, but I wish it were a little more... gentle. And consistent."

"Welcome to Texas," Quinn said. "Perpetual drought interrupted by intermittent flooding."

"Perfect for farming," I said. "Whose idea was it to settle here, anyway?"

"People looking for cheap land?" Quinn replied with a grin.

"Well it isn't anymore, unfortunately," I replied. With more wealthy Houstonians and Austinites buying up properties in Buttercup, prices were going up fast. I was glad I'd bought my grandmother's farm when I did. I was hoping to expand my acreage at some point, although to be honest, I was having a hard enough time keeping up with what I had. I didn't know how I was going to handle anything larger.

"Speaking of land," Quinn said, as if reading my mind, "I heard a rumor that Faith Zapalac was over at your neighbor's house the other day."

"What? Which one?"

"Dottie Kreische's," she said. "I haven't heard anything

else about it, but Dottie's son Jessie had lunch with her at the Blue Onion the other day. It looks like Dottie may be moving to Sunset Home in La Grange."

"I hope she doesn't move," I said. I'd enjoyed getting to know Dottie since moving to Buttercup. I remembered her from when I was a child visiting my grandparents—she'd always worn a sunny smile on her broad face, and had plied me with cookies when I went next door to borrow a cup of sugar for my grandmother—and we'd had tea many times since I'd taken over the farm. Later, when I was older, I'd babysat her kids, Jessie and Jennifer, from time to time. She'd told me lots of wonderful stories about my grandparents; it would be a real loss if she left. "I knew she wasn't doing well, but I hate that she's got to leave. She's spent her whole life on that farm."

"I know," Quinn agreed.

"There's no way she can stay here?"

"I don't know; I'm just reporting what I heard. I know she has a home health aide some of the time," Quinn said.

"You mean Eva?" I asked. Eva Clarke was a caring woman in her midthirties, and whenever I'd visited and seen her, she'd seemed to treat Dottie like family. "She's great; she really cares for Dottie."

"I've seen her with Dottie at the Blue Onion sometimes. Unfortunately, Dottie's reached the point where she needs someone with her all the time."

"That's too bad," I said.

"I know," Quinn agreed, grimacing. "Anyway, although I hate to think of breaking up the property, if she decides to sell, it might be a good opportunity to pick up some acreage right next door."

"If I can afford it," I said, feeling a touch of anxiety at the thought of deciding whether to expand my little operation.

I'd come into a few windfalls recently, but most of that money had gone toward renovating the little house. As the rain pounded on the roof, I found myself feeling gloomy.

At least the cistern and the well would fill up, I told myself, trying to look for a silver lining. It was early in the season for tornadoes thankfully, but I still eyed the clouds nervously. I'd lived in Texas my whole life, and thankfully, I'd never yet seen a tornado. People said you could hear them coming, but the rain on the metal roof was so loud I wasn't sure how you could. "How do you know if a tornado is coming? I've heard the sky is supposed to turn green, but I've never seen it."

"It looks kind of green now, actually," Quinn said, glancing out at the sky. As she spoke, my phone buzzed with an alert. I grabbed it, and my stomach clutched. "Tornado warning."

"Where?"

"Here," I said, staring out the window. "What do we do?"

"Do you have a root cellar?"

"No," I said. "But the little house does."

Quinn scooped up Chuck.

"What about Dottie?"

"Let's go check on her," Quinn said. We ran out to my truck without stopping for rain jackets. Puddles had already formed on the driveway, the sandy soil turning to mud. As I turned at the end of the driveway, Quinn jabbed a finger at the sky above my neighbor's house. "What's that?"

A funnel cloud was forming.

Adrenaline coursed through me as I turned the key. It took two tries to start it; when it finally caught, I gunned the engine. "It's almost on top of the house," I said. I was crazy to keep driving toward it, but I hated to think of what might happen to my neighbor if we weren't able to get her to safety in time.

The tires spun briefly as I punched the gas; a moment later, the tires grabbed and we lurched forward.

The funnel cloud was heading right toward the house. Would we make it in time?

Or would all of us be caught in the middle of a tornado?

2

A small, beaten-up Honda was parked next to Dottie's old Ford truck.

"That's Eva's car," Quinn said as we slammed the truck's doors shut and sprinted to the front door. We didn't bother knocking; I threw open the front door and raced inside. "Dottie! Where are you?"

"I'm in here," answered a wavering voice I recognized as Dottie's. "Is Eva with you?"

We hurried to the small bedroom, where Dottie was tucked into her bed.

"There's a tornado," I blurted. "We have to find a place to go. Is there a cellar?"

Dottie eyes widened. "Tornado?" Although her body was deteriorating, my neighbor's mind was still sharp. "I saw the weather, and I told Eva we might be in trouble. She went out about an hour ago; I don't know where she's gone."

"Her car's here," I said. "We didn't see her, though. But we've got to find a safe place for you; is there any shelter here?"

"There's an old root cellar beside the house," Dottie said. "Do we have time to get there?"

"I don't know," I said, "but it's our best bet.

Together, Quinn and I got Dottie into her wheelchair and raced to the front door, Chuck at our heels. It sounded like a freight train was bearing down on the little house.

"Where is it?" I yelled as the wind whipped my hair into my face.

"Over there!" Dottie said, pointing to two peeling wooden doors in a shallow frame under a pecan tree about ten yards from the house. The rain felt like buckshot against my face.

"We'll have to carry her down!" I said as we raced over to the two doors. Quinn flung the doors open, exposing dusty steps. The wind brought a smell of earthiness as Quinn and I lifted the chair. The steps were uneven, and not wide enough for two of us and the chair.

"I'll take the bottom!" Quinn yelled, descending a few steps and grasping the chair just above the front wheels. Chuck followed her down.

A branch flew off the pecan tree with a loud crack; as I took the first step, it glanced off my head. I didn't dare look up.

Together we plunged into the earthy darkness, about six steps down; the roof was so low there was no room to stand. We got the chair down, and Quinn and I hurried back up to fasten the doors. One was flapping in the wind; as I reached to grab it, it slammed into my arm. The train noise was so loud I couldn't hear myself think. I could hear someone yelling behind me, but the wind snatched the words away. Another branch came down as I threw myself onto the door, grabbed the handle, and pulled.

The wind was fierce. It took all my strength to pull the

door shut; as I did, the last thing I saw was a mailbox flying through the green-tinted air.

"How do we brace it?" I yelled to Dottie.

"There's a two-by-four at the bottom of the steps," she yelled back, her reedy voice wheezy.

Quinn carried it up to me; as she clung to the doors, trying to keep them from blowing open, I threaded the two-by-four through the metal handles. With a brief prayer that the doors would hold, we stumbled down the now-slick steps and retreated to the deepest part of the cellar.

It smelled of earth and decay and dust and rain.

And fear.

"Did it hit the house?" Dottie asked, gripping my hand with her bony one. I had to put my ear right next to her mouth to hear her.

"Not that I saw," I told her, squeezing her hand. "But it was close." As I spoke, there was a loud crack, and the doors shuddered. The pecan tree? I wondered. Or part of the house? Chuck quivered against my legs, and as I stroked him with my free hand, my mind strayed to Blossom and Gidget and Hot Lips and the new babies and the rest of the animals. Were they safe in the barn? What would I come back to? Or would I come back at all?

I said a silent prayer as the wind grew louder and more things slammed into the doors. Would they hold? Or would the wind rip them off and then pluck us out of our hole in the ground?"

Dottie squeezed my hand so hard her rings bit into my flesh, and I could feel Chuck whining as he trembled next to me. The roaring intensified, and the doors rattled so hard I was sure they were going to fly off or crack open.

And then the sound began to fade. The doors settled down; the rain still beat against them, but the sound of the freight train was receding. Which direction was it going? I wondered, but there was no way to tell. Was my farm going to be okay? Dread gathered in my stomach.

"How long do we stay in here?" I asked.

"Until we can't hear it anymore, to my mind," Dottie said, her voice strained and tired. "They double back sometimes."

"Have you been through one of these before?"

She nodded, her bony hand still gripping mine. "Twice. Tore up the pasture and some of the trees by the creek. The second one landed a pecan tree on the corner of the house. It took six months to repair it."

We sat in silence, listening as the rushing sound faded into the distance. It was only fifteen minutes or so, but it felt like an hour; the waiting was excruciating.

The rain was still pounding down in waves, but the eerie wind was gone when I climbed the steps and pulled out the two-by-four. Bracing myself for what might be on the other side, I pushed back the doors.

The pecan tree was gone... all that remained was a stump half-twisted out of the ground. I felt a twinge for the ancient tree... but at least the house was still standing. I turned to look toward my farm. Although there was no sign of the twister now, the tornado's destructive path had cut a swath straight toward Dewberry Farm. My heart clutched in my chest; were my animals okay?

"It went right over us," Quinn breathed. "Thank goodness the doors held or we could have been on our way to Kansas."

"The house?" Dottie asked, voice quavering, from behind me. "Is it still there?"

"It's there," I reassured her, assessing it. The porch had suffered some damage—two of the posts had buckled, and the porch roof was askew—but the house looked intact. I looked back at Quinn. "Let's get Dottie back into the house. Can you keep Chuck and stay here with Dottie while I go check on my animals?"

"Of course," she told me. "Let's get her up to the house, and then you can go."

"What do we do about Eva?" I asked.

"I'll look for her while you're checking things out. Then we'll look together."

"Thanks," I said. Ten minutes later, I closed Dottie's door behind me and raced to the truck; Chuck and Dottie were safe inside the house, and Quinn was making tea. The rain had soaked me to the bone, but I didn't care. I hurled myself into the driver's seat, threw the truck into reverse, and a moment later, raced down the driveway at top speed, headed for home.

Assuming I still had one.

THE HOUSE I'd spent my childhood summers visiting was still standing when I crested the gravel driveway, and I breathed a sigh of relief.

The barn was there, too... but the roof was twisted up at the front left corner. My breath caught in my throat; were Blossom and Hot Lips and Gidget and the rest of my little flock all right?

I pulled up outside the barn and threw the truck door open, not bothering to shut it before sprinting over to the damaged barn.

The siding had been ripped off the front of the structure, and the metal roof looked like someone had tried to peel it off. Inside, the cows and goats were huddled in the back corner, wide-eyed and agitated. Relieved, I did a quick head count... only to discover that two of the kids, Thistle and Cinnamon, were missing.

Carrot, their mother, was bleating loudly and sniffing around, looking for them. I glanced back at the open corner of the barn, feeling sick to my stomach. Had they been caught in the tornado?

I hurried out of the barn and scanned the pasture. The tornado had ripped up a line of vegetation and the storm had flattened the rest, but there was no sign of the brown-and-white goats. The fence was down, though. Was it possible they'd escaped after the tornado went by?

More than anything, I wanted to go looking for them, but I had to make sure everybody else didn't break free while I was out searching the pasture. I was examining the destroyed corner of the barn when a truck turned into the bottom of the driveway. With a surge of relief, I recognized Tobias's truck.

I was still guarding the corner of the barn when he pulled up next to my truck. "Everyone okay?" he asked as he slammed the door behind him and jogged over to where I was standing.

"Thistle and Cinnamon are missing," I said, "and the fence is down."

He scanned the interior of the barn. "We've got to get them secured; and this barn doesn't look like it's in great shape."

"How?" I asked.

"Rope," he said after a moment. "We'll tether them. The goats will probably chew through it, but at least it will buy us a little bit of time. Do you have harnesses for them?"

"I do," I said. "Thank goodness they didn't blow away."

We spent the next twenty minutes securing the cows and goats. Tobias spoke in soothing tones that calmed the anxious animals down... everyone but Carrot, that is, who was frantically searching for her kids.

"We'll find them," Tobias assured me.

"I didn't check the chickens," I realized when we had the last goat tethered.

"Go check," he said. "I'll see what I can do about the fence."

"Thanks," I told him, and hurried out to the chicken coop. Although the hens were all tucked away in a corner, burbling anxiously, everyone appeared to be accounted for. I refilled their food and water and stepped out of the coop, my heart sinking as I surveyed the fields Quinn and I had attempted to protect with row cover.

My livestock might be okay, but my vegetables weren't. The tomato cages were scattered around like children's toys, and the fledgling plants they'd been protecting had been flattened or torn out of the ground. The row cover we'd carefully laid down had been ripped up and strewn all over the place, and the baby squash plants I'd been nurturing had been shredded.

From the perspective of vegetables, it looked like a total loss.

I took a deep breath and tried to look on the bright side. The tomatoes and squash hadn't been in that long; it was a little late to replant, and the yield might not be as high, but it wasn't irrecoverable. I hurried back to the barn, trying not to think of how much work had been lost—and how much I would have to do to clean things up. Tobias, bless him, was busy righting fence posts and stapling wire.

"How bad's the fence?" I asked.

"I can patch it for now," he said, "but it could use some work. The barn's going to take a bit to repair, too. How are the chickens?"

"All accounted for," I said, "but my vegetables are toast."

"All gone?"

"Pretty much," I told him. "I'm going to have to start over again."

He grimaced. "Is it too late in the season?"

"It's a little late," I said, "but not too late. At least I hope not." I was past the time for maximum yields, I knew that, but maybe I could still eke out something... "The timing's bad, though. I heard some of the land next door might be up for sale. I'd like to pick up some extra acreage, but that might be difficult if I'm short on cash." I sighed. "The main thing is, the animals are okay and my house is still standing. And I'll probably get a little extra income from the rental house."

"Dottie is selling?"

"Her kids want to move her to an assisted living place in La Grange."

"That's too bad," he said. "I hope your new neighbor is as nice."

"The way things are going, it's likely to be a weekender."

"There do seem to be a lot of those here recently."

"I kind of feel funny about renting out a guesthouse, myself," I said. "I want Buttercup to be more than just a tourist destination, or a weekend spot for city folks."

"It's not like you're not here year-round, and contributing to the community." Tobias sighed. "But it's hard to lose the old-timers. Dottie's spent her whole life here. The prospect of moving has got to be hard."

"I know. I wish there were some way to keep the home health aide twenty-four seven. Quinn and I went over when the storm started, to make sure she was okay. In fact, I should probably get back there; I kind of left Quinn stranded."

"Are all your buildings all right?"

"The porch roof of the little house is a bit messed up, but overall everything seems to be okay."

"So both you and Dottie managed to avoid the worst," Tobias said, his eyes straying to the fence line between my property and my neighbor's. "It'll be sad to see her go. So many of the old-timers seem to be dying off lately." He turned and smiled at me. "I'm glad you came back."

"Me too," I said with a smile.

He gave me a quick kiss and said, "Why don't you go check on Quinn? I'll finish patching the fence, and then we can go look for the kids."

I'd almost forgotten about Thistle and Cinnamon. "Think they're okay?"

"I'm sure they are," he said. "They probably just got separated. We'll find them."

"I hope so," I said.

"Go get Quinn, and we'll track them down."

"Got it," I said as he righted another fence post. "And thanks."

"Anytime," he said as I kissed him on top of the head and then hurried to the truck.

3

When I got back to Dottie's house, Quinn was inspecting the porch roof. Chuck ran over and jumped up to greet me; I bent down and stroked his silky ears, then gave his warm, wiggly body a hug. "Everyone here okay?" I asked as I released the poodle.

Quinn tucked a red curl into her bandanna and nodded. "It's going to take a little bit of work to fix the roof, but it could have been a lot worse. I got Dottie back into bed, and made us chicken salad sandwiches. How's the farm?" she asked.

"The house is standing, but two of the kids are missing," I said.

Her face clouded. "Which ones?"

"Thistle and Cinnamon," I said.

"Oh, no... they're only a month old!"

"I know. Tobias thinks they haven't gone far; I hope he's right, and they weren't sucked up by the storm. Carrot's really upset."

"I'll bet," she said. "Everything else okay?"

"The barn's a bit messed up, and the row cover was a loss; it might have protected against hail, but the wind took it all off. All the crops are flattened; I'll have to start over."

Quinn winced. "Flattened?"

"The wind ripped everything up," I said. "The tornado must have touched down right on the corner of the barn."

"I'm so sorry, Lucy."

I sighed. "It's a setback, but at least most of the animals are okay, and my house is still standing. It's still early in the year; I can replant."

"I'll help," she said, glancing back at the house. "For starters, let's see if we can get some sandwiches together, and then one of us can go look for those kids."

"And Eva," I said. "Her car was at Dottie's, but she'd been gone for an hour when the tornado came."

"That doesn't sound good," he said.

"I know," I agreed. I had a bad feeling about Eva's disappearance, but I hoped I was wrong.

THIRTY MINUTES LATER, I'd combed my property, but there was no sign of Thistle and Cinnamon.

Or of Eva.

Quinn had stayed with Dottie, and Tobias had started his search in the other direction. Since I hadn't heard from him, I was guessing he was out of luck, too. I'd called Quinn to check on Dottie and see if Eva had come back. Still no word. Eva wasn't answering her cell phone, and she hadn't come back to the house.

"I hope she didn't get caught in the tornado," Quinn said.

"Me too," I said. "It's weird that she was gone an hour

before the storm came through, though. That doesn't seem like her; from everything I've seen, she was devoted to Dottie."

"I know," Quinn agreed. "I can't imagine she would have left her for so long. Especially with a storm coming in."

"It was a pretty fast-moving storm, though. Maybe she got caught by surprise?"

"Maybe," Quinn said. "But why did she leave in the first place?"

"That's a very good question." I sighed. "I'm about to go through the gate into Dottie's property," I told her. "I'll keep an eye out. Are you still okay?"

"I'm fine," she said. "Apparently the cafe didn't get hit—the tornado missed downtown altogether—and Fannie's going to go let Pip out into the back yard for me. Take all the time you need."

"Hopefully we'll find everyone before that!" I said, trying to ignore the little coil of fear unfurling in my stomach as I hung up the phone and stepped through the gate.

DOTTIE'S PROPERTY was lush and beautiful, with the exception of the narrow track left by the tornado. Several cedar trees and a few oaks had been corkscrewed out of the ground, showing where the twister had come through. A storage building had also been in the track; what looked like a rusted-out tractor and maybe even a spinning wheel were now exposed, thanks to the back wall being ripped off. Whose spinning wheel was it? I wondered as I walked by. Dottie's?

Still, most of it was intact. Dottie's family had raised

cattle for decades, but unlike many ranchers, who had grazed their land until there was nothing left but compacted soil and prickly pear cactus, they had always rotated their livestock and tended to the ecosystem to keep the pastures healthy. I knew Dottie had also been interested in restoring native grasses and plants; in fact, because she loved to spin, dye, and knit wool, she had completely fenced off an area dedicated to native tall-grass prairie plants and native plants traditionally used for plant dyeing. The area she had reseeded with little bluestem, Indiangrass, buffalograss, and sideoats abutted my property. She'd allowed me to harvest some of the seeds and scatter them on my own land; I had a few bunches of bluegrass coming up here and there, and hoped I could keep the goats from annihilating them. A few purple prairie verbena popped up here and there among the grasses, as did baby bee balm and evening primrose, all three of which I knew Dottie had used for dyeing. I'd wanted to gather some for my own natural egg-dyeing packets, but it was too early in the season. Next year, I told myself.

I looked at the soft green growth coming up through last year's bleached grass. Next year... if there was one. If Dottie sold her property, would the new owner preserve what she'd worked so hard to create, or just run too many cattle over all of it until her years of husbandry were destroyed?

Pushing the thought out of my mind, I scanned the area for any sign of the kids... or Eva. "Thistle!" I called. "Cinnamon!" And then, a little bit louder, "Eva!"

Nothing.

I pushed forward onto Dottie's land, avoiding a small huddle of cattle gathered around a stock tank. Live oaks dotted the rolling pasture, along with a few cedar trees, and several bright green sycamores and cottonwoods were clustered down by the creek, which I could hear rushing along its banks after the rain. I walked along the fence line, a few yards into Dottie's property; I was planning to double back and walk the property in lines so that I covered everything.

Another torn-up pecan tree lay in my track. As I stepped over it, a glint of metal caught my eye. I reached down and picked up a large, tarnished silver locket attached to a slender, broken chain. As I did, a chill swept over me. I looked around, wondering if there'd been a sudden breeze, but the grass around me was still. I flipped open the locket, exposing a lock of faded yellow-orange hair. Whose was it? One of Dottie's ancestors? I wondered.

This wasn't the time to speculate, though. I slipped the locket into my pocket to show Dottie, then poked around with my foot at the base of the tree to see if there was anything else I'd missed. There was nothing obvious, but I made a mental note of the tree's location and moved on, far more worried about Eva and the kids than searching for artifacts exposed by the storm.

I continued to call as I approached the creek. The ground was squashy underfoot, making me glad I'd stopped to grab my boots. I looked for signs of footprints, either human or goat, but saw nothing. Either they'd come this way before the rain, or I was barking up the wrong tree, so to speak.

The kids had to be out there somewhere, I told myself as I skirted a small clump of cactus and followed the slope down to the creek. The vegetation changed as I got closer; the grass gave way to clumps of dewberries and a few young frostweed plants, as well as several vines I recognized as poison ivy. I skirted the vines as I made my way down to the banks, praying that Thistle and Cinnamon hadn't been washed away by a torrent.

The water in the swollen creek had risen sharply, completely submerging some of the plants on the muddy banks.

"Thistle! Cinnamon! Eva!"

As I called, I thought I heard a bleating noise farther downstream. I strained my eyes and called again, but heard and saw nothing. Grabbing the slender trunk of a young hackberry for balance, I made my way down the bank, calling and listening for any response. Then I heard it again.

I hurried through the underbrush, trying to locate the source of the sound. "Thistle! Cinnamon!"

A faint bleat answered me. It was Thistle, looking tiny and drenched, lying on her side. She was caught under a fallen branch, her legs covered in water.

"I'm here," I told her as I reached her. Her eyes rolled in her head, panicked, and she bleated, but she was so exhausted she could barely lift her head. "I've got you," I told her as I lifted the branch, praying it hadn't broken her back.

To my relief, Thistle flailed her legs, struggling to get to her feet. I scooped her up into my arms, holding the wet, shaking body to my chest. "Where's your sister?" I asked, scanning the banks and listening. "Cinnamon!" I called. "Cinnamon!"

I picked my way up the bank, searching for Cinnamon with the shivering kid clutched to my chest, but there was no sign of Thistle's sister. My stomach churned with worry for the baby goat, who had always been full of spunk and curiosity. Had she been washed away by the rising waters?

I was about to turn back to Dewberry Farm when a flash of something pink caught my eye. "We'll go back in a moment,"

I murmured to Thistle, holding her close as I stepped over a snarl of sawbrier. Whatever it was was half-submerged... had somebody lost a jacket in the storm? I wondered. I pushed a few branches out of the way and then sucked in my breath.

It wasn't a lost jacket.

It was Eva.

4

"Eva!"

I stumbled forward toward the woman's prone form, Thistle clutched to my chest. Eva's face was pale and turned to the side, and one arm bobbed in the strong current. I half-slid down the bank toward her, churning up mud and young plants as I crouched by her head and sat down in the mud, Thistle nestled into my lap.

"Eva!" I called again, hoping she'd respond to her name. Her eyes were half-open, seemingly sightless. Her hand lolled in the brown water, and I felt a shiver of foreboding course through me as I touched her neck, searching for a pulse.

She was cold.

I reached in my pocket for my phone and dialed Tobias, hand shaking.

"I'm coming up empty," he said. "How about you?" he said when he picked up.

"I've got Thistle, but Eva..."

"Oh, you found her. She came back?"

"No," I said. "I'm down by the creek. She's..." I looked

down at the young woman's prone form. Her chest was still, and her face was pale and waxy. "I think she's dead."

I DIDN'T KNOW how long I'd been sitting by the creek when Tobias came crashing through the undergrowth. "Lucy," he said as I looked up. "Are you okay?"

"I'm... I don't know," I said.

He kissed me on top of the head and then turned to Eva, feeling for a pulse. He grimaced, shaking his head. "She's gone. We need to call the sheriff, unfortunately." Then he turned to the little body curled up in my lap. "She looks exhausted," he said, examining her. "But I don't see any physical trauma."

"I found her in the creek," I said. "Under a heavy branch."

"No sign of Cinnamon?"

"None," I said.

"Well, she may still turn up," he said, turning back to Eva. "What I don't understand is, how did Eva end up here?"

"I was wondering the same thing," I said. "Maybe she accidentally went into the creek during the storm and got carried away by the water?"

"Speaking of water, it's still rising," Tobias observed; he was right. The bank I was sitting on was quickly being swallowed by the creek. "I'm afraid we're going to have to move her before Rooster gets here."

"Do you really think it will matter?" I asked.

"Probably not. Although we might get lucky and get Deputy Shames."

"I tried," I said. "I called the sheriff's office while I was waiting for you. Opal wasn't there, so it's going to be the luck of the draw, I'm afraid." Opal womanned the front desk at the sheriff's office, and had become something of an ally over the past year or two.

"Do you have Thistle?" he asked as I clambered to my feet.

"I do," I said, still cradling the trembling body. As I made my way up the slippery bank, Tobias stood behind Eva and lifted her by her armpits, sliding as he maneuvered her up the bank. Her arms flopped around and her head lolled back.

"Tobias," I said. Despite the spring weather, a sodden wool scarf was wrapped around her neck. As it shifted, I pointed to what appeared to be bruises on her neck.

"That doesn't look like an accidental fall," he said.

"And I don't think the tornado did that to her."

"No," he said as he tugged her away from the water and gently set her down on the bank. Now that the scarf had shifted, I could see a ring of dark bruising on her pale neck.

"Someone strangled her with her own scarf, didn't they?" I said in a soft voice, shuddering.

"And then dumped her in the creek, it looks like," he said. "There are leaves and branches in her hair."

"So someone wanted it to look like she got caught by the tornado and drowned in the creek?"

"Maybe," Tobias said. "Thing is, though, drowning victims have water in their lungs."

"And they don't have bruised necks." As I turned away from the body, something caught my eye. "What's that?" I asked, pointing to a sodden piece of paper protruding from Eva's pocket.

"It looks like a name," he said.

I pulled my phone out of my pocket. "What is it?"

"The paper's torn, so there's only a piece of it. Looks like something Holding... maybe Cup?"

"Cup Holding? That's kind of random," I said. "Anything else?"

"I don't want to touch her more than I have to," he said.

"Take Thistle for me," I said, handing him the kid. I wrapped the hem of my wet T-shirt around my hand and felt Eva's pocket. "No phone here," I said, and moved to check the other pocket. It was also empty.

"Did you see her phone at the house?" Tobias asked.

"No," I replied. "And we called it a couple of times; no one picked up." I checked her jeans pockets; they were also empty.

"So someone strangled her, then took her phone," he said.

"Either that or she lost it in the water," I said.

"Maybe," he said. It was too murky to tell.

"Maybe the police will have better luck," I suggested, but I didn't have much confidence. I looked at Eva's pale face again. Who had killed her?

And why?

BY THE TIME Deputy Shames showed up, the water had risen another two feet, and we'd had to move Eva farther up the bank. Tobias had given Thistle a quick exam; she was shaken, but should be okay. I just wished we could find her sister. And that we could somehow bring Eva back.

"Storm victim?" the deputy asked as she tramped through the pasture with a camera-laden officer I didn't recognize at her heels.

"It doesn't look like it," I said, pointing to the scarf and bruises on her neck.

She grimaced. "Bad news. Is Dottie okay?"

"Quinn's with her," I said. "Eva apparently left the house not long before the tornado hit. I was out looking for missing kids and found her."

"Do you know when Eva was last seen alive?"

"According to Dottie, she went out about an hour before the storm and never came back."

"Was she going to meet someone?"

I shrugged. "Dottie didn't know. She must have taken her phone with her, unless she left it in the car. We called her from Dottie's house, but didn't hear it ring."

"Any sign of it out here?"

"No," I said. "But I haven't done much searching, to be honest.

"We'll have to cordon off the area," she said. "Obviously, we don't have a coroner's report yet, but I'm fairly comfortable saying this looks like a homicide."

"Let us know if we can do anything to help," Tobias said.

"I'll come ask you some questions in a bit," she said. "I know you've got to get that little one back home to her mama. It's usually a futile request in Buttercup, but all I ask is that you don't say anything about what you found here," she advised us.

"We understand," I assured her. "Let us know if you need anything."

"Any idea who might have wanted to do her in?" she asked bluntly.

"No," I said, shaking my head. Eva had seemed well liked, from what I'd seen.

"Well, she rubbed someone the wrong way," the deputy observed. "And I aim to find out who. I'll be by to talk to Dottie in a little bit."

"I'll have to go back to the house," I said. "I don't want to lie; can I tell her Eva's gone?"

She nodded. "Please tell her I'll be by with questions as soon as I get some more investigators out here," she said. "And that I'm sorry for her loss."

I glanced at Tobias, who reached to touch my arm. Thank goodness Deputy Shames had turned up instead of Rooster. Eva might be gone, but at least we had a competent law enforcement officer on the scene.

For now, anyway.

WE WERE CLEARED to go within a half hour of the deputy's arrival. "I'll take this one back and get her cleaned up and reunited with her mama," Tobias told me as we walked up the creek bank, away from what was left of Eva. An ambulance had pulled into the driveway. I hated to have to share the news. And I still didn't know what had happened to Carrot's baby.

"What do you think happened to Cinnamon?"

"I don't know," Tobias said solemnly. "I'm hoping she found her way back home. If not, we'll put out an alert and keep searching."

"Yes," I said. "That's all we can do, I guess. In the meantime, I guess I have to go tell Dottie."

"I'm so sorry." He kissed me on the forehead when we got to the fence. "See you in a bit?"

"Call me if Cinnamon turns up, okay?"

"Of course," he said, sheltering the little kid as he ducked through the fence. I watched him walk back to the barn for a moment, feeling thankful to have met such a good and caring man, before turning toward Dottie's house to break the bad news. My fingers trailed the bleached stalks of last year's little bluestem as I walked. Would it still be here next year?

Quinn was waiting for me on the porch when I turned the corner of the house.

"What's going on?" she asked.

"We found one of the kids," I told her.

"That doesn't explain the ambulance."

I sighed. "And Eva."

"Is she okay?"

"The kid is," I said in a low voice. "Eva... not so much."

Quinn's eyes widened. "What happened?"

"I'm not supposed to say anything about the details, but it looks like she was the victim of foul play."

"You mean somebody killed her?"

I nodded.

Quinn's hand moved to her throat, echoing what must have happened to Eva while Quinn and I were putting down row cover. I shivered, thinking that whoever had killed Eva had probably been close enough to see Quinn and me working out in the field.

"Did you happen to notice anyone out and about at Dottie's when we were working?" I asked.

"You mean when we were putting down row cover?"

I nodded.

"Not that I remember," she said.

I sighed. "Is Dottie awake?"

"I just got her settled in the living room and turned on a game show," she said. "Time to break the news, eh?"

"Unfortunately, I think we have to."

"I'll go with you," she said. Together we walked into the little house's living room, where the cheery sound of *Jeopardy!* blared from a small tube-style television. Dottie was ensconced in a faded green velour armchair; a gold couch and a love seat from the same era formed a TV-viewing ring.

Although I was sure the subfloor was hardwood, a faded brown carpet stretched from wall to wall. Framed pictures of her children, from babyhood to young adulthood, covered the walls, and a series of more recent baby pictures adorned the top of the TV. I knew Dottie loved her family.

My neighbor looked up from where she was sitting in the chair, a blanket over her lap despite the warm spring temperature. She looked frailer than I remembered, and I hated to have to tell her what I knew. "Any luck finding Eva? Or those missing baby goats Quinn told me about?" my neighbor asked, eyes sharp.

"Sort of," I said, sitting down on the couch across from her recliner. "I'm afraid I've got some bad news."

"What? Did the goats pass? I'm so sorry, Lucy."

"It's about Eva," I said. "She didn't make it through the storm."

Dottie stared at me for a moment, then seemed to deflate, sinking back into the chair. "I can't believe it," she murmured. "It couldn't be..." Her color was alarmingly pale.

"I know it's a shock," I said. "Can I get you anything? A glass of water?"

"Do you need to lie down?" Quinn asked.

"No..." Dottie said, seemingly lost in a world of her own. Then she gave herself a little shake. "What happened? It was the storm, right?"

I hesitated, then said, "I'm not sure."

"Foul play," she croaked. "No. It couldn't be," she repeated. "Can't be."

Couldn't be what? I wondered. Was she just upset that Eva had died, or did she suspect something else?

5

"I'm so sorry," Quinn said, and I reached down to squeeze Dottie's hand.

"Deputy Shames is going to be by to ask you some questions in a little bit," I said in a quiet voice.

"Are you sure it wasn't just the storm? And why do the police want to talk to me?" She looked afraid, somehow. Quinn and I exchanged glances.

"We're here," Quinn said, hurrying over and kneeling beside her chair. I took the other side, taking Dottie's fragile hand in my own and giving it a squeeze. "Where's Jessie?" she asked. "I have to talk to my son."

"I don't know," I told her softly. "We'll give him a call."

"No," she said. "No. I was wrong... never mind. I'm fine." She took a deep breath and seemed to marshal herself. "I'll be just fine. Poor girl. It must have been one of her boyfriends. She had so many."

"Boyfriends?"

"Oh, yes," Dottie said, seeming a little frenzied. "She liked to make them jealous. I told her it wasn't a good idea, but..."

"Do you know their names?"

"Oh, there were a few of them. I heard her talking on the phone with Gus..." she said.

"Gus? You don't mean Gus Holz, do you?"

"Yes, that's the one," she said. "She was planning a dinner with him."

My stomach clenched. Today was just getting worse and worse, I thought to myself. Gus had started going steady with my friend Flora Kocurek over the Christmas holiday. Had he been two-timing her with Eva? If so, I knew Flora would be devastated. I glanced at Quinn, who looked equally grim.

"Eva was talking about him just the other day," Dottie continued. "I'll be sure to tell the deputy. Poor thing," she repeated. "She was just doing her best." She squeezed her eyes shut, then opened them wide. "Tea. Is there any tea?"

"I'll get you a glass," Quinn said. "Sweetened or unsweetened?"

"Just a pack of the pink stuff, please," she said. "Eva keeps... kept it in a jar by the coffee maker. Although I suppose I won't have a coffee maker much longer, will I?"

"What do you mean?"

"I just don't know if I can keep the place up," she said. "Even with Eva..."

"I heard a rumor that Faith was looking at listing the place," I told her. "I was hoping it wasn't true."

"Nothing's been decided," she said.

"You're really thinking of selling?" Quinn asked from the kitchen.

"I don't want to," she said, her frail frame seeming to shrink further, "but Jessie thinks it's best. It'll help pay for the assisted living. I have some money put away, but most of it's tied up in the farm."

"We'd hate to see you leave. There's no way you could get another home health aide?" Quinn asked.

"Jessie's pretty insistent," she said. "My boy loves me. He'll do what's right for me." She sounded brave, but I could see her lower lip trembling as she spoke. I didn't know much about her son Jessie's motivations, but I had a feeling that Dottie's interests weren't the only ones being considered when it came to the potential move.

"Even if he's insistent," I said, "you've got to be sure it's the right thing for you."

She sighed. "I just don't know anymore. I thought maybe I shouldn't do it. I hate the thought of the place being taken over and turned into one of those hobby ranches. But now, with Eva..." Her mouth snapped shut. "I shouldn't talk about this."

Quinn was about to answer when the doorbell rang.

"I'll get it," I said, and a moment later, opened the front door to Deputy Shames.

"Did you tell her?" she asked as I let her in the door.

"We broke the news, yes."

"She take it okay?"

"As well as can be expected," I told her.

The deputy nodded, her face grim. "Did she say anything?"

"She seemed to think it might have been due to a romantic entanglement," I said, "but that's it. She's moving to an assisted living center in La Grange soon, apparently."

"I imagine sooner now that Eva's gone." Deputy Shames grimaced. "Thanks for taking care of her. Do you know how to get in touch with any family members, now that Eva's gone?"

"She talked about calling her son. I know she's got a son and a daughter."

"Should probably get in touch with them," the deputy said.

"I'll see what I can do.

∽

As Deputy Shames talked with Dottie, Quinn fixed some glasses of iced tea while I adjourned to what was left of the front porch to make a few phone calls. I couldn't reach Dottie's son Jessie, but her daughter Jennifer answered on the second ring.

"Oh, no... that's horrible! Is Mom okay?" she asked.

"She's shocked, of course," I said. "If there's anything I can do to help Dottie stay here comfortably, let me know. I worry about transitioning her to a nursing home; she mentioned that might be in the works."

Jennifer was silent for a moment, and I could hear the sound of children bickering in the background. "Kayla... knock it off," she told someone in a stern voice, then said, "Nursing home? Mom never said anything about a nursing home. She always swore she'd never leave the farm unless it was in a pine box."

"Well, it sounds like she may be changing her mind. A few minutes ago, she told me she was talking with your brother about selling the place and moving to an assisted living center in La Grange."

"My brother? You're kidding me. That..." She stopped and took a deep breath before continuing. "She never said anything to me about it," Jennifer replied, the bitterness in her voice palpable. "But she always did think he hung the moon, and he always did make the most of it. I'm going to call and give him a piece of my mind. He can't make these decisions for her, especially not without consulting the rest of the family!"

"I'm sorry to be the bearer of bad tidings," I said.

"No," she told me. "It's not your fault. I'm glad you told me... I should have guessed he'd be up to something like this." She put her hand over the phone and admonished Kayla again, then got back on. "Sorry about that. I'll head up there as soon as my husband gets off work; I can't leave the kids alone, and I'm not sure I want to bring them if she's that upset."

"One of us will stay with her until you get here," I assured her.

"Thanks," she said.

I gave her my phone number and assured me she could call me anytime. "Is there anything else I can do?"

"No," she told me. "You've been amazing. Mom always liked you... she had us late, and loved when you'd come by and help out with us kids."

"That's right!" I said. "I remember when you and your brother got into the sugar and covered the kitchen floor with it."

"Remember who took the fall for that?"

Jennifer had, as I recalled.

"He always had her wrapped around his little finger," Jennifer told me. "I thought I'd made my peace with it, but I guess I haven't just yet."

"I'm so sorry," I told her. "I hope to see more of you."

"I'll give you a ring," she said. "And call me if you hear anything else about the whole real estate thing, please?"

"I don't know that I'll hear anything, but I promise if I do, I'll let you know."

"Thanks," she said, and we hung up.

"Jennifer won't be here until six thirty or seven," I told Quinn when I walked back into the house. "I probably need to go back and make sure that fence is tight before nightfall, but I don't want to leave her."

"I'll stay with Dottie and wait until she gets here," Quinn said, handing me a glass of iced tea.

"Thanks. I'll see if I have a casserole in the freezer I can drop by for them," I said. Deputy Shames was still talking with Dottie, so we headed back onto the front porch. "What do you think of the Gus Holz thing?" I asked as I settled into one of the painted rocking chairs.

"I don't know," Quinn said, sitting down next to me and biting her lower lip. "I hadn't heard anything about Gus seeing anyone else, and word usually travels fast in Buttercup."

"Have you heard from Flora recently?"

"I haven't," she said. "But I'm not to inclined to say anything to her about it."

"Me neither," I agreed. "But it worries me."

Quinn took a sip of her tea and pushed a wayward curl out of her eyes. "She's had pretty rotten luck in the boyfriend department," Quinn said. "I hope we haven't steered her in the wrong direction. Quinn wasn't wrong; Flora's previous boyfriend had turned out to be a particularly bad apple. When Gus Holz had shown interest at the Christmas Market, Flora had been nervous, but based on what we knew about the bachelor rancher, Quinn and I had encouraged her to go for it. Now, she was completely smitten... I'd even heard her broach the "M" word. *Had* we steered her wrong?

I pushed that worry from my head; with Eva gone,

Cinnamon missing, and my crops devastated, I had more pressing concerns. "Want to come over to dinner later?" I asked Quinn. "I have to head back in a few, but when Jennifer gets here, let me know; I figure she and Dottie can join us, or if they're not feeling up to it, I can drop something off for them, and then you and I can eat together."

"That sounds good," she said. "Do you have anything on hand to make? I'm happy to help."

"I think I've got some enchiladas in the freezer I can heat up. Plus, I picked up some shrimp this week; I was going to make shrimp and goat cheese quesadillas."

"Sounds delicious," she said. "Only thing is, I don't know what time I'll be free."

"It's pretty quick to whip up," I said. "I might even make a margarita or two."

"I'm definitely in, then," she said, grinning.

"Thanks for helping out at the farm today, by the way."

"I'm just sorry it didn't help," she said. "You'll be okay, you think?"

"I think so. I just wish we could find Cinnamon," I said.

"Oh, Lucy, I'm sure she'll turn up."

I wasn't so sure, but I appreciated Quinn's optimism.

6

Tobias had patched the fence while I was gone; although his truck was no longer in the driveway, he'd left me a note on the kitchen table.

Thistle's doing okay for now; just check on her and call me if you see any trouble. No sign of Cinnamon yet but will put the word out. Fence should hold for the night. We'll reinforce it this weekend. Had a few emergency calls so had to head out, but will be in touch when I can. XXX OOO Tobias

I smiled as I read the note—Tobias could have texted, but a handwritten note was so much nicer—then headed out to check on Thistle. She was nestled close to her mother. Carrot was still showing signs of anxiety, no doubt over the loss of Cinnamon, but seemed comforted to have at least one of her kids back with her. The rest of the animals seemed to be past any lingering trauma from the tornado; the cows kept nudging me, hoping for treats, and when I checked on the chickens, they were out in the yard wondering where their lunch scraps had gone.

After calling a few neighbors to check on them and see if anyone had seen our missing kid, I spent the next hour picking up row cover as I walked around the farm calling for Cinnamon. The thin fabric had been shredded by the storm and distributed all over the property, along with torn leaves and uprooted vegetables. As evening drew close, I abandoned the growing pile of row cover and headed down to the creek once more, hoping that maybe I could find the poor baby goat. The water was still rising, making a rushing sound that reminded me a little of the sound of the tornado. I shuddered at the thought of it, and sent a small prayer up for Thistle. And Eva.

Someone had killed Eva Clarke, I reflected as I gathered another tangled mass of row cover from where it was tangled in a tree, piling it up a ways away from the flooded creek.

But who? And perhaps just as importantly, why?

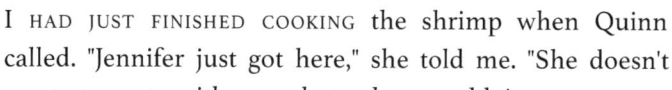

∼

I HAD JUST FINISHED COOKING the shrimp when Quinn called. "Jennifer just got here," she told me. "She doesn't want to eat with us, but she wouldn't say no to enchiladas."

"I popped them in a while ago, and they're ready to go," I said. "I'll be over in a few. Is Dottie doing okay?"

"Actually I think she might have been doing better before her daughter turned up," Quinn said in a hushed voice. "They're not exactly bosom buddies, I gather."

"What's going on?" I asked.

"Jennifer's not happy about the whole nursing home

thing," Quinn said. "And she seems to think her brother isn't acting in Dottie's best interest."

"Let me know if you hear anything that might help explain what happened to Eva," I said.

"Will do," she promised.

Ten minutes later, I was back at Dottie's front door with a warm tray of enchiladas. I could hear the raised voices even before I hit the doorbell.

"How goes it?" I asked as Quinn answered the door.

"Not good," she answered as I walked into the front hallway. "I'm kind of afraid to leave them alone together."

"What are they arguing about?"

"Jessie's plan to put his mother in a nursing home," Quinn said as I set the pan on the stove. "Why don't you come say hello? Maybe it will help."

"I'm not sure it's safe," I said as Dottie raised her voice again from the other room.

"I don't want to discuss it!" Dottie said as Quinn and I walked into the living room. When she saw me, she closed her mouth. Her daughter, Jennifer, was standing next to her, arms crossed, her full face flushed.

"Jennifer?" I asked.

Her face softened when she saw me. "Lucy," she said, coming over to give me a hug. Jennifer was much rounder than I remembered, and looked tired. She wore jeans and a faded pink T-shirt, and smelled like sunblock and talcum powder. "It's been so long!" she said as she gave me a squeeze.

"It has," I said. "I'm glad to see you, even though the circumstances could be better."

"You have no idea," she said ominously.

"Hey, why don't you help me with the enchiladas?" I

asked, glancing at Dottie, whose mouth was set in a thin line.

"I'd love to," she said, looking relieved at the prospect of a brief break from her mother, and followed me into the kitchen as Quinn fussed with Dottie's blankets.

"What's going on?" I asked quietly.

She let out something between a sigh and a snort. "I asked him about what you told me. Turns out my idiot brother talked her into giving him power of attorney. He's trying to convince her to go into a nursing home and sell the farm. And he did all of it behind my back!"

"I'd think that would be something the whole family would decide together," I said.

"You'd think, wouldn't you?"

"You've got kids, I hear."

"Two," she said. "They're four and three; they run me ragged."

"I'll bet," I said.

She ran a hand through her short hair. "I haven't had as much time as I'd like to check on Mom. I'm regretting that now; Kayla had an ear infection last month that just wouldn't go away, and then Liam got a stomach bug, and I meant to come up and check on her and I didn't. And... well, Bill and I have separated."

"I'm so sorry," I told her.

She burst into tears. "I just feel like I'm letting everyone down all over the place."

I gave her another hug, and she sobbed into my shoulder.

"Life happens," I told her. "Marital strife is hard. It's harder still when you've got little kids."

"I haven't even told my mother," she said. "I'm afraid she'll be disappointed in me. She's always been disappointed in me. And now she probably thinks I've abandoned her, which is why she's relying on Jessie so much."

"I'm sure she knows you love her."

"Sometimes I wonder," she said, glancing at the doorway to the living room. There was a look of sadness in her eyes, and I could see the little girl I'd watched all those years ago. "She was so fond of Eva, as if she were the daughter she'd always wished she'd had..."

"I'm sure that's not what it was," I said.

Jennifer shook herself. "Of course not. I just hope it's not too late to make it right."

"You think she doesn't want to go to the home?"

"I think he's convinced her she doesn't have enough money to stay here," Jennifer said. "She thinks he's an amazing money manager, but she has no idea what's really going on."

"What *is* going on?"

"He spends every cent he gets; have you seen the car he drives?"

"No," I said as I pulled back the tinfoil on the enchiladas.

"It's a brand-new Cadillac Escalade."

I let out a low whistle. "Aren't those like seventy-five K?"

"They are," she confirmed. "He bought it for himself at Christmas... but I know he got laid off from his job three months ago. I found out from a mutual friend; he hasn't told me about it himself."

"And you think this sparked the push for Dottie to sell the house?"

Jennifer nodded. "I hate that I even have to bring this up, but I really think he just wants access to the money from the sale of the house and land. He spends every cent he gets... I'm sure he doesn't have any savings, and I don't know how he's making the payments on the house and the car. If I didn't know better, I'd wonder..."

"Wonder what?" I asked.

She flushed. "Nothing. It was an awful thought."

"Are you wondering if he had something to do with what happened to Eva?" I asked.

"She never liked him," Jennifer said. "He told me more than once that she was poisoning Mother's mind. It's a ridiculous idea, though," she said, waving a hand as if pushing the thought away. "I shouldn't have even thought it, much less said it out loud."

"It's okay," I said. "You're upset."

"I am," she said, swiping at her eyes and then looking around at the small kitchen. The tiled countertops and wood floors hadn't changed since those summers I'd spent in Buttercup as a child and then a teenager, and the row of porcelain chickens on the windowsill looked just like they had when I babysat Jessie and Jennifer all those years ago. "I just can't believe he could do something like this. We grew up here. This is our family's history!"

"It's not done yet," I reminded her. "Have you talked to him?"

"He says it's none of my business," she said, looking defeated. "He refuses to talk about it. Said if Mother wanted to involve me, she would."

"And what does Dottie say?"

"She says he's handling everything, and she doesn't know any more than that."

I sighed. "That's got to be so hard. Did you tell your mother about the layoff?"

"Frankly, I don't think she'd believe me."

"It's got to be hard to make those car payments on unemployment," I said, thinking out loud. "Is he married?"

"He is," she said, "but his wife Melody works as a receptionist."

"So she's not making the big bucks."

"You could say that," she said with a twisted smile. "I have no idea how they're making mortgage payments, either. But Mother just tells me that he knows what he's doing, of course. Or else why would he be driving that fancy car?"

I sighed. "That's got to be so frustrating."

"It is," she said. "I've been eating Snickers bars like mad. By the way, those enchiladas smell amazing. Chicken and verde sauce?"

"Yup. I used tomatillos," I confirmed. "And probably too much cheese."

"You can never use too much cheese," Jennifer said with mock gravity.

"I like your philosophy," I said with a grin. "Seriously, though. What can I do to help you?"

"Just... talk to her. Maybe suggest she look at the finances herself. She was always good about money when we were growing up. Thrifty."

"I remember she used to use old milk cartons to protect her tomatoes," I said, "and she grew all her own vegetables and canned them."

"She did," Jennifer said proudly.

I sighed. "I'll see what I can do. I'm sorry you have to go through this."

"Thanks," she said, and looked down at the enchilada pan. "I should probably get Mother fed and put to bed. It's been a long day."

"It has," I agreed.

"Thanks so much to you and Quinn for coming over to make sure she was okay," she said.

"Of course," I said, reaching out to squeeze her shoulder.

"That's what neighbors do. And I'll do everything I can to help your mom out."

"Thanks," she said, giving me a hug. "You always were my favorite babysitter."

I laughed. "I just can't believe you've got kids of your own!"

"Let me show you!" she said, and whipped out her phone. We spent the next few minutes scrolling through photos of her children—a little girl with a wonderful, mischievous smile and a boy with enormous blue eyes—and by the time we headed back to the living room, Jennifer was in slightly better spirits.

"Call us if you need us!" I reminded them both as Quinn and I headed for the door.

"Thank you so much," Jennifer said as she dished up enchiladas. "I'll get the pan back to you tomorrow!"

"Take your time," I said as Quinn and I headed into the soft spring evening. The air smelled fresh and clean; it was hard to imagine that a violent storm had come through just hours before.

And that Eva Clarke had lost her life just a few hundred yards away.

7

When we arrived at my little farmhouse, Chuck just about bowled Quinn over with kisses.

"Hey, Chuck," she said, squatting down to pet him. He wagged so hard he almost knocked himself over. "He seems to be doing okay. How's Thistle?"

"We should probably go check on her," I replied. "I just wish I knew what happened to Cinnamon. I called all the neighbors, but nobody's seen her."

"I'm sure she'll turn up," Quinn said in a tone of voice that was not entirely convincing. "What did you and Jennifer talk about, anyway?" she asked as she peeled off her muddy boots and set them on the porch.

"Well, she told me her brother got laid off a few months ago. And now he's got power of attorney and is pressuring Dottie to go into a home and sell the house."

"Is Dottie in that bad a shape?" she asked.

"I don't know," I said. "But it doesn't sound good. Did you manage to get in touch with him today?"

"I called him, but he didn't answer," she said. "If Dottie goes on and on about Jessie all the time, I can see why Jennifer might be a little miffed."

"I have a feeling Jennifer suspects her brother might have done in Eva."

Quinn's eyes widened. "Really?"

"She said Eva was against Jessie's crusade to get Dottie to sell the house. When I wondered out loud if he might have had a reason to want Eva out of the way, she kind of flushed and said she felt guilt even thinking about it, but..."

"We should probably let Deputy Shames know about the situation with Dottie," Quinn suggested. "Of course, it would kill her if her son really was a murderer."

"But if he is—and I'm not saying he is—doesn't Eva deserve justice?"

Quinn sighed. "Man... what a question. Families can be tough, can't they?"

I thought about the jealousy in Jennifer's voice when she talked about Eva... as if Eva were the daughter Dottie had always wished she'd had. As much as I hated to think it, it occurred to me that Jessie might not be the only one with a motive to get rid of Eva. I shook myself, as if that would rid me of the thought, but it still lingered. She said she'd been home with the kids... but could that have been a story?

With Chuck on her heels, Quinn followed me into the kitchen and sat down at my kitchen table. "Need any help?" she asked as I pulled down a mixing bowl and grabbed a container of goat cheese from the fridge.

"I've got it," I said. "It's a pretty easy recipe. Want a margarita?"

"I'd love one," she said. I set the goat cheese down and reached into the freezer for some ice cubes.

"Can you get me the tequila and triple sec from the bottom of the pie safe?" I asked as I scooped some of the limeade into the blender.

"Got it," she said, opening the bottom cabinets and retrieving the two bottles. I measured in a few jiggers of each, added some ice, and grabbed the dewberry puree I'd made from some frozen berries the day before. "How do you feel about dewberry margaritas?" I asked.

"That sounds heavenly," Quinn said. I juiced a lime into the blender and dumped in some ice, then measured out some of the dewberry puree—I'd cooked the frozen berries down with some sugar and lemon juice and then strained the mixture—along with generous amounts of tequila and triple sec. As the blender whirred, I took two margarita glasses I'd picked up at last year's antique fair and rimmed them with sugar. A moment later, I filled them with the dark purple slush.

"Cheers," I said as I handed her a margarita. We clinked our glasses, and when she took a sip, Quinn's eyes widened. "This is amazing," she told me. "I need the recipe."

"I'll send it over," I told her. I opened a bag of chips, poured some salsa verde into a bowl, and set both in front of my friend as I got back to working on the quesadillas.

We talked about Dottie and Eva as I mixed shredded Monterrey Jack and goat cheese, then retrieved a few sprigs of the cilantro that had survived the storm and chopped them up. "How long had Eva been helping Dottie out?" Quinn asked as I added the cilantro to the cheese mixture along with some fresh garlic, salt, and pepper.

"At least a year," I said. "Eva seemed devoted to her."

What I don't understand is, why would she make a change like that if everything was going so well?"

"According to Jennifer, Jessie convinced Dottie that the finances weren't looking too rosy. And assisted living places aren't exactly cheap," I pointed out. I would give him the benefit of the doubt for now, I decided.

Quinn furrowed her brow. "If most of Dottie's equity is in her property, maybe she couldn't afford to stay without accessing it."

"She mentioned that might be the case. But why not do a reverse mortgage?" I asked.

Quinn shrugged. "I'm not the one making the decisions," she said. "You'd have to talk with Dottie. But something tells me she wouldn't want to discuss it. To hear her talk, her son Jessie is the financial wizard."

"That's not what Jennifer said. He's driving a brand-new Escalade, but apparently he just got laid off. Which gives me the feeling it's not Dottie who came up with the idea of selling the property."

"Maybe he is pushing her to sell," my friend said. "I don't know. I just know that I'll be sad to lose Dottie."

"All kinds of bad news today," I said, taking a long sip of my margarita. The tangy lime and dewberry were a perfect foil to the tequila, and although I wasn't a big drinker, today had been the kind of day that almost required a little pick-me-up.

"What else is wrong?" Quinn asked.

"Well, there's Eva, of course. And Cinnamon. And I'm worried about Flora now, too."

"What about her?"

"Remember what Dottie said this morning? We told her Gus seemed like a solid guy; what if we were wrong?"

"Flora and Gus are both adults," Quinn reminded me. "They're in charge of themselves. From everything we knew,

Gus seemed like a good option, and when she asked our opinions, we gave them. Besides," she added, "Dottie was upset. And who knows where she was getting her information from?"

"True," I said as I heated a pan on the stove and laid out four fresh tortillas. I took another sip of my dewberry margarita—it was the perfect slushy mix of tart and sweet, and went down far too quickly—and added the cooked shrimp to the mixture, then divided it among the four tortillas. I "sandwiched" each of them with another tortilla, then melted a knob of butter in the pan and carefully added the first quesadilla.

The kitchen soon filled with the mouthwatering scent of browning butter and goat cheese, with only a tinge of the briny aroma of shrimp. Quinn and I were both salivating by the time I finished the last quesadilla. I quartered them using a pizza cutter and set them on the table with the salsa verde while Quinn set the table.

A few minutes later, my friend and I were sitting in front of a cheesy, shrimpy stack of melted goodness. "I love these," she said through a mouthful of quesadilla.

"Me too," I mumbled as salsa verde dripped down my chin.

"Oh—did I mention I did one of those DNA tests the other day?"

"No," I said.

"I got the results back. I always thought I was mainly Czech and Irish, but it turns out there's a big chunk of German in there, too."

"Wasn't one of your grandmothers adopted?" I asked.

"She was," Quinn said, looking melancholy. "I wish I knew more about my family from before. Who were they?

I'm thinking of doing Ancestry.com to see if I can find some relatives. The family I have is small; I don't have any siblings, and my parents were only children, too. And now they're both gone."

"And all the stories with them. I'm so sorry," I told her.

I took another sip of margarita. As I put the glass down, there was a sudden drop in temperature in the kitchen, and something cold pressed against my leg. Chuck whined nervously; I bent down to pet him.

"Chilly all of a sudden," Quinn said.

"I thought maybe it was the margarita, but I don't know," I said, putting my hand in my pocket to figure out what felt so cold. It was the locket; I'd forgotten about it.

"I found this at Dottie's today," I told Quinn as I pulled it out of my pocket and set it down on the table. Despite being in my pocket, the metal was cold. It was still streaked with mud, and the tarnish made it almost black.

"That looks old," she said, reaching out for it.

"There's a picture inside," I said. "It looks familiar, but I can't place it."

She peered at it. "And some hair," she said, poking at the curled-up, faded lock. "It's kind of creepy."

"I know," I said. "I found it at the base of a tree that got twisted out of the ground. I need to give the locket to Dottie, but if she's okay with it, I might look around to see if anything else got turned up."

"This land has so much history we know nothing about, doesn't it?"

"It does," I said. "It's part of what makes it so magical."

"Yes," Quinn said, taking another sip of her margarita. I followed suit. Despite the good company and delicious food, I still felt hollow. Poor Eva would never have another quesadilla again. And I still had no idea what had happened to Cinnamon.

∽

AFTER QUINN LEFT, I walked the property one more time, looking for Cinnamon, but there was no sign of her. I knew the odds were against her, but I prayed that somehow someone had found her and was taking care of her. I checked on the rest of the animals; the fence had held, and everyone was settling in for the night, none the worse for wear after the day's excitement. I wrapped up a few more candles to take to the Easter Market, which was starting this week, and watered the herb starts, thankful that at least they had survived the storm. Then I took Chuck out one last time so he could do his business before settling into my cozy bedroom with a skein of marigold-dyed wool yarn.

Before Dottie got sick, she'd been an avid wool-dyer, and had kept a few sheep for their wool, becoming an expert wool dyer, spinner, and knitter. She'd once told me she'd learned the craft from her mother, who'd learned from her own mother. I could sense her disappointment that her Jennifer hadn't shown interest, and was delighted when I inquired after the plants. With her permission, I'd experimented with a few for my egg-dyeing experiments.

As Chuck settled in beside me, I started a row on my thick knitting needles, hoping to fall into the Zenlike state I often enjoyed while knitting. Calm was escaping me this evening, though. I was worried about Dottie, and poor Eva, and Cinnamon, and the crops I'd have to replant...

It wasn't all bad, I reminded myself. Eva was gone—that was a tragedy—but I was still okay. All the buildings, including the renovated house, had survived, and it was early enough in the year that I'd still get some yield this summer. Besides, milk production would be up with more goats and cows on the farm, so I'd have more cheese to sell. Plus, with the new hives I was hoping to set up soon, I'd be less reliant on outside suppliers for beeswax and honey.

But my mind kept circling back to Cinnamon... and Eva.

After about an hour, I put down my knitting, turned off my light, and drifted to sleep.

At some point during the night, I was back in the farmhouse kitchen with my grandmother, helping her make bread. I was a child again, and my grandmother wore the same checked apron she always wore, her hair pulled back away from her sweet, crinkled face. She let me dust the board with flour before she turned out the dough out and began to work it, humming as she kneaded. The room smelled of yeast and flour and my grandmother's lavender perfume, and her eyes crinkled as she smiled at me. "You have to keep at it if you want it to come right," she said, and I wasn't sure if she was talking about the dough or something else.

She handed me a scrap of dough and I slipped it into my mouth. A moment later, there was a knock at the door. "You keep kneading," she said. "I'll be right back." I reached for the dough and tried to knead it, but it was like Silly Putty, not dough. It just wouldn't budge. As I fought with it, women's voices drifted to me from the front of the house; although I strained, I couldn't hear.

After a long while my grandmother came back to the kitchen, carrying a long, deep basket, almost like a bassinet. "That was Liesl from next door," she said. "She wanted me to ask you to patch things up for her. Make it come right."

She handed me the basket. I put down the dough and took it from her; inside was a skein of yellow wool and a needle, and the locket I'd found in the field next door. And then suddenly I wasn't a child anymore.

"I found that locket yesterday," I said.

"You did," my grandmother agreed.

I stared down at the contents of the basket, baffled. I looked up at my grandmother, suddenly small again. "What do I do?"

"You'll know," she said, and put a hand on my head. "Liesl will help you."

"Who's Liesl?" I asked, but before she could answer, the dream fragmented, as dreams do, and I was alone in my bedroom, with Chuck sleeping fitfully at my feet.

THE NEXT MORNING DAWNED GRAY, and way too early, as far as I was concerned. I dragged myself out of bed to face the carnage that was the remains of my farm, hoping against hope that Cinnamon might have made it back to the barn.

She hadn't.

I promised everyone I'd be back to milk them soon, then headed to gather eggs from the chickens—assuming they'd laid any, after all the excitement yesterday. I tried not to look at the flattened rows of vegetables, but it was impossible to ignore them... or the work that would be required to replace the missing crops. I'd planted almost everything from seeds I'd started, but I'd have to replace much of it with transplants. Between that and the cost of fixing up the damage to the little house, I didn't like to think about the state of my bank account, much of which had already been emptied doing renovations on the historic house.

The latch of the chicken coop was open when I got there, and the door stood slightly ajar. The hair stood up on the back of my neck. Had my chickens been chickennapped?

I pulled the door open to find the hens all huddled together in the corner. The back wall of the coop was plastered with broken eggs, and a message scrawled in something that looked like blood.

MIND YOUR OWN BUSINESS... OR ELSE.

8
———

I did a quick head-count; everyone was there, but my hopes for a morning omelet was, obviously, dashed. That was the least of my worries, though. Who had threatened me? And if I didn't "mind my own business," what exactly was going to happen?

And what had set someone off? Was it to do with Eva? Or was it because I'd been asking questions about Dottie?

I cleaned up the eggs and fed the chickens. The letters, thankfully, had been spray-painted—no blood—but it would still take some work to get rid of. I'd have to paint over them; I couldn't imagine looking at that horrible message every morning.

I rinsed the egg off the wall, found a padlock for the chicken coop, and then took care of the rest of my morning chores with a heavy heart. It was almost ten by the time I'd finished my morning rounds. I wanted to stay home and keep tabs on everyone, but I had errands to do—including buying vegetable starts to replace what I'd lost—so I made sure Chuck was safe in the house and locked the door before climbing into the truck. It took a few tries before the engine caught—another thing to take care of, I thought—and I backed out of my gravel parking spot with reluctance, worried about leaving my farm... and wondering if maybe I should buy a shotgun after all.

Just in case.

∼

THE TORNADO WAS the talk of the town when I stopped by the Blue Onion on my way to pick up replacement plants from Greenleaf, a wholesale nursery not far from La Grange.

The little cafe was stuffed with locals, sipping iced tea, eating quiche and swapping gossip.

"I heard it took the roof of the Marks's barn clean off," Mildred Ehrlich was telling a friend as I walked into the cafe.

"Livestock okay?"

"They are, miraculously," she said. "But I heard the storm sucked all the feathers off his chickens. They're walking around naked!"

"That I have to see," Mildred said. She looked up and noticed me, and her eyes brightened. "Lucy," she said. "Heard the storm went through your place yesterday. Everything okay?"

"My crops are destroyed, I'm afraid, and I'm still missing a kid," I told her, "but except for a little bit of damage, the buildings and the rest of the livestock are all okay, so I'm counting my blessings."

"Heard you were the one who found poor Eva," said her companion, Gretchen Hoffman.

"That was me," I confirmed.

"If you don't mind my asking, what happened to her? Just between us, of course."

I resisted the urge to roll my eyes. Mildred was a more efficient distributor of news than the local paper, the *Buttercup Zephyr*, by about a factor of ten. "I'm not supposed to talk about it," I said.

"Heard it was foul play," Mildred said with a gleam in her blue eye.

I shrugged noncommittally. "It's very sad. She seemed like a very nice person, and it's got to be hard on Dottie."

Mildred shook her head. "I'm not surprised, to be honest. I always told her, if you stick your nose into other people's business, you're gonna get yourself burned."

Again, that was rich coming from a woman who was pretty much a central trunk of Buttercup's very active grapevine. But I put on a polite smile and asked, "What do you mean? Had she gotten anyone into trouble recently?"

"Oh, she was always nosing around, finding things out, and then telling other people about it 'for their own good.' Got herself fired over at Sunset Home in La Grange a while back, too."

"She did? When was that?"

"A year or two ago," Mildred said. "She got real close with one of the residents. Managed to convince him that his daughter was trying to take all his money. Maybe she was, too; he ended up writing his daughter out of the will before it all got squared away. They fired her, of course."

"That sounds horrible," I said. "Do you think it was real, or was she trying to... I don't know...."

"Get his money?" Gretchen asked. She shook her bouffanted head. "I don't think so. Eva may not have had the best judgment, but she has... well, *had* a good heart."

"She grew up without a momma, and her dad was on the

bottle the whole time, so I think she just got in the habit of tryin' to take care of everyone all the time," Mildred volunteered. "Too much, if you ask me."

"Do you know if she was stirring anything up recently?" I asked.

"So you *are* investigatin'," Mildred said. "I thought so."

"I'm just curious," I said.

"I know she's dating that newcomer to town," she said. "Edward Bartsch. Works down at the wool store. Thinks he's an artist of some sort."

"Is... or was... she seeing anyone else, do you know?"

Mildred and Gretchen exchanged glances. "Maybe," Gretchen allowed. "But I don't like to gossip."

"I won't say a word to anyone," I promised.

"Well," she said, leaning forward, "I heard she was at a Mexican restaurant in La Grange with Gus Holz a week or two back.

My heart sank. Maybe there was something to what Dottie said, after all. "Why were they in La Grange?"

"You'd have to ask them," she said, "but they were havin' dinner at Guadalajara."

"Poor Flora," Mildred said, shaking her head but looking slightly gleeful. "Thank goodness she's got her mama's money to keep her warm. She hasn't had much luck in the romance department."

"It was just dinner," I said, too shortly.

They gave me a pitying look.

"But back to Eva," I said. "Anyone else you know who might have had ruffled feathers?"

"Well, she was sore about the Sunset Home problem."

"Really?"

Mildred nodded. "She ran into one of the folks who run the home; she was here at the Blue Onion last week with a prospective family member, I think. Eva said a few words that a lady can't repeat, right in front of the family member, and then stormed out, madder than a wet hen."

"And no idea what they were arguing about?"

"Eva wasn't a big fan of how they were runnin' the place, it seems," Mildred said. "Said she was plannin' on puttin' a stop to it, and that she'd die rather than put a family member in that place."

"What was the nursing home person's name?"

"I don't remember," she said. "She's not from Buttercup, I do know that."

"It's a shame what happened to Eva," Gretchen said. "She and Dottie seemed awfully close."

"Unless you brought up Dottie's son Jessie," Mildred said. "That boy can do no wrong as far as his mother is concerned. Speaking of Jessie," she said, "he's here right now."

"Is he?" I asked.

She pointed over to the corner of the cafe. I recognized our local real estate agent, Faith Zapalac, but I could only see the back of her dining companion's head.

"Always felt bad for Jennifer. She spent her whole life tryin' to get her momma's attention, but Dottie only had eyes for Jessie."

"Mind you, it's not Jessie who's makin' sure Dottie gets to her doctors' appointments and all. I only ever see Jennifer."

"Are you sure about that?" Mildred asked in a low voice. "He's been in Buttercup a few times recently," she said. "I saw his truck parked a few doors down, across the street from the Town Green."

"What do you know about him, anyway?"

"He's got some job down in Houston," Mildred said. "Comes back for a day or two at Christmas, and sends the kids up for a week or two in the summer, but doesn't come back up here nearly as much as his sister does." My eyes strayed to the table in the corner again. Faith and her dining companion seemed in deep conversation.

A moment later, Quinn hurried into the dining room through the swinging door to the kitchen. "Lucy!" she said when she spotted me. "Any word on Cinnamon?"

"None yet," I said.

"What's Cinnamon?" Mildred asked.

"One of my kids," I said. "She went missing during the storm yesterday. I'd like to think someone found her and took her in, but I'm afraid she may be lost." My heart twisted as I said it. I knew keeping livestock meant dealing with losses, but it was hard when you were faced with one directly.

"Poor thing," Mildred said. "I'll keep an ear out, see if she turned up somewhere. Your barn been vandalized yet, by the way?"

I blinked, surprised. Was I not the only one? "Funny you should ask. It was, just this morning, actually. Someone broke into the chicken coop, broke all the eggs, and spray-painted a message on the wall of the barn."

"Real sorry to hear that. Somebody's been spray-paintin' barns the past few weeks. Lettin' Ed Zapp's chickens out, too."

"I heard about the chickens," I said. "I'm glad mine are okay... but tell me more about the vandalism. What was spray-painted on the barns?"

"Big letters of some kind," she said. "Some kind of nonsense. Not sure what they mean."

There hadn't been any letters in the coop. A cryptic message, to be sure, but not letters. Was it the same culprit? I wondered. Whoever it was, it was creepy.

"Think we have some kind of gang startin' in Buttercup?" Mildred asked.

"That would be a surprising development," I said.

"Well, you never know. Keep your eyes open."

"I will," I said. "Please let me know if you hear of anything... or if you remember anything about Eva."

"If it was foul play," Mildred said in a low voice, "does it bother you that it was practically on your doorstep? I mean, you're right there, and living all alone..." She shivered.

"I've got Chuck to protect me," I said, but in truth her comment did send a frisson of fear through me.

"Dogs are good, but a shotgun's better," Mildred advised.

"I'll think about it," I said, not mentioning that I'd already given it some serious consideration just that morning. "Thanks for chatting. I'm going to go check in on Quinn."

"Good luck finding your stray kid," Mildred called as I headed across the cafe to where Faith and Jessie were huddled. Faith was wearing a particularly bright shade of red lipstick and a plunging neckline, which Jessie appeared to be appreciating. Was this her new marketing strategy? I wondered. She let out a throaty laugh at something Jessie said as I stopped by their table.

"Hi," I said, and they both jumped.

"Good morning, Lucy," Faith said, reaching down to adjust her neckline. She was Buttercup's primary real estate agent, with a nose for business and not a lot of scruples; she and I had tangled before.

"Hi, Faith. Hi, Jessie," I said. Jessie hadn't changed a lot from when I babysat him as a kid, only much larger. I remembered him having round cheeks and a perpetual pout; although he now sported new sideburns and a beard, neither the round cheeks nor the pout had changed. His belly spilled over his jeans, and was only barely kept in check by a button-down shirt. He looked like a heart attack looking to happen. "I just wanted to say I'm sorry about what happened to your mom's health aide, and to tell you I'm happy to help in any way I can." I smiled. "It was good of you to come up and look after her."

"I always look after her," he said defensively.

I blinked, surprised. "Of course," I said. "I know Dottie's terribly broken up about Eva—so am I— but that's got to make things difficult for you, too. Is there anything I can do to help?"

"I've got things under control," he said.

"I'm glad to hear it. Looking to buy a place in Buttercup? It'll be nice for her to have you close by; I know how much she loves you."

Jessie looked to Faith as if he needed help answering the question. "We're conducting other business at the moment," Faith said sharply, even though I had addressed Jessie.

"I heard your mom might be putting her place up for sale," I said to Jessie.

Faith tightened her lips.

"I don't mean to pry," I said, although that wasn't entirely true, "but if you do, would you let me know? I might be interested in picking up a few acres."

"We'll keep that in mind," Faith said, which told me the rumors were true. "But parcels usually do better when they're sold intact. Of course, if you're interested in purchasing the entire property..."

"Keep me posted," I said, and looked at Jessie. "I'd hate for that strip of native plants your mom's been working on restoring for all these years to be destroyed; I'd be happy to maintain it."

He said nothing, only fiddled with his wedding ring.

"So, is Dottie going to Sunset Home in La Grange?"

"That's family business," he said.

I got the hint. No more questions about Dottie. "Again, I'm so sorry about Eva," I said. "Did you know her well?" I asked.

"She was an employee," he said, but his face colored.

"Thanks for stopping by to chat, Lucy. Now, if you'll excuse us," Faith said, her expression suddenly hard, "we've got business to attend to."

I glanced down at the papers on the table; the words "Brokers Market Analysis" jumped out at me before Faith pulled the papers together.

"Right," I said. "Good to see you both."

He nodded dismissively. They both waited until I was out of range before she opened the folder again, I noticed, and Faith sent me a sidelong glance, as if making sure I hadn't installed a spy camera.

Quinn looked up from the sink, where she was rinsing lettuce, as I walked into the kitchen.

"Any luck finding Cinnamon?" she asked.

"No," I said. "But someone vandalized my chicken coop." I told her about what had happened.

"I'm so sorry, Lucy; I know this is not what you need. I hope they find the culprit soon," she said. "This has been going on for a month."

"Whoever it was threatened me. MIND YOUR OWN BUSINESS... OR ELSE. They smashed a bunch of eggs, too."

"What on earth is that supposed to mean?" she asked as she shook the colander with the lettuce.

"I don't know," I said. "Maybe because I found Eva?"

"You do have a reputation for solving murders," Quinn pointed out. "Any other news?"

"I had a chat with Mildred Ehrlich."

"She likes to have the skinny on everyone. Find anything out about Eva?"

"Dottie was right; Eva she had dinner with Gus Holz in La Grange," I said.

Quinn winced. "That doesn't sound good. Still," she said, "It was just dinner. Right?"

"I hope so," I said. "She was dating Edward Bartsch, too."

"I've seen him around town."

"He works at that new wool store, Buttercup Weavers and Knitters; he just moved to town a few months ago, right?"

"He did," she agreed. I'd been to the new wool store a few times, and had spent far too much money there; I knew I'd met him a few times. "I wonder how Deputy Shames is getting on with the investigation?"

"I hope she's the one getting on with it," I said. "And not Rooster."

"He's so lazy he's not going to take over anything that someone else has volunteered to do," Quinn said. "Besides, he's too busy trying to keep Lacey from running to Austin to live with her mother and daddy."

"I thought that was getting better," I said.

"It was," Quinn told me. "But he stayed out all night last night. Apparently he was playing poker and drinking beers and didn't want to drive, but he forgot to call to tell Lacey that. By the time he got home, she'd gone to Austin."

"Well, at least she's not just putting up with it. I guess."

"We'll see what happens," Quinn said. "But hopefully he'll be busy enough that he keeps his nose out of the investigation. Every time he gets involved, he slaps handcuffs on the most convenient person."

"And he's always wrong."

"Exactly," Quinn said.

I sighed. "I'm headed out to Greenleaf Nursery to pick up some replacement plants in a few, but I thought I'd stop in to see if you need a hand with anything."

"Early rush is almost over, and I've got plenty of help," she replied, nodding toward her two helpers in the kitchen. "If I get a chance, maybe I'll swing by tonight and help you out."

"That would be great," I said, "but only if you have time. I know you're busy. How are things at Peter's, by the way?"

"A little bit of hail damage," she said, "but nothing like what you're having to deal with."

"I'm glad," I said. "I guess it was just my chance to win the lottery this time. It could have been a lot worse, though."

"True, but that doesn't mean you still don't have work to do."

"I know. I'm just trying to look on the bright side," I told her. "You sure you don't need me here?"

"I'm good," she said. "Go get your replacement plants, and be careful, okay? I'll come by to help this afternoon if I can! Oh—when I do, I want to show you some things I found in a box in the back of the closet."

"Like what? Shoes?"

"No," she said. "Old papers that were my mom's. The box fell off the shelf yesterday—it was so weird—and it looks like there may be some adoption stuff from my grandmother in there. I was hoping you could help me figure it out."

"I'd love to," I said. "But don't you need to get ready for the Easter Market?"

"I've got help coming in to finish the last of the baking this afternoon," she said. "How about you? Are you ready?"

"As ready as I can be, considering. I'd love to see you and

go through the papers," I said, and gave her arm a squeeze. "I should be home in a couple of hours. Thanks for offering to help. You're a good friend."

"So are you, Lucy," she said, a smile crinkling her eyes.

BY THE TIME I turned onto Kramer Road toward Dewberry Farm, the bed of my truck filled with seedlings, the sun was dropping toward the horizon. As I crested a rise in the road, I was surprised to see a familiar white SUV at the base of my neighbor Dottie's driveway. I slowed down, feeling my stomach clutch.

I rolled past the house just in time to see Faith Zapalac pounding a For Sale sign into the ground next to the driveway.

9
———

I pulled over to the side of the road and got out of the truck. "Dottie's selling already?" I asked Faith, who was wearing tight white capri pants and bright red heels.

"She is," said Faith coolly, turning to face me. Her lipstick matched her heels. "If you want a parcel, you should probably put in a bid soon."

"I thought it was still up in the air, the whole selling thing."

Faith shrugged. "I guess not. She listed it today."

I sucked in my breath. "Is she here?"

"She's already gone to La Grange."

"Gone to La Grange? As in moved?"

"Jessie picked her up and took her this morning," she said. "Right before we had lunch."

My stomach churned; there was something off here. "Do you have her number at the new place?"

"No," she said. "You might want to touch base with Jessie."

"I will," I said, and hurried back to my truck. I grabbed

the phone and dialed Quinn; she didn't answer, but I left a message. Then I called Jessie: same thing. The truck was slow to start; it took me a few tries, and I made a mental note to get it checked out soon. Once the engine finally roared to life, I put the truck in gear and headed back to Dewberry Farm, feeling a deep sense of loss. I couldn't believe my neighbor was gone permanently, and that the place she'd spent her whole life was about to be put up on the auction block. Who was driving this decision? Was it really Dottie? Or was her son railroading her into selling up and moving to a retirement home miles from her lifelong home?

~

Despite everything going on with Eva's death and the missing kid and Dottie's farm going up for sale, the first morning of the Easter Market was calm, clear and cool. I ran a load of laundry through the washer as I hurried through my morning chores, thankful that my vandal hadn't been back, then quickly pegged the wet laundry to the line before loading up the truck.

I busied myself setting up my stall at the market, trying not to worry about all the other things going on. I'd gotten up early to take care of the farm chores before loading up the truck and driving into town. Quinn hadn't had a chance to come over the previous evening, but I'd made good progress putting in the new plants, and was hoping to do some more when I got home this afternoon.

Thanks to the tornado, I didn't have much in the way of produce to offer, but I did have plenty of beautiful products I hoped would sell well. In addition to my normal lineup of beeswax candles, jams, and bar soaps, I'd been making colorful egg-shaped soaps for weeks; they were displayed in little nests I'd woven from the dried grapevine down by the creek. I'd also put up a small "tree" from which I'd hung decorative eggs I'd blown and dyed naturally, using wax to create intricate patterns. Beside them were small kits of natural dyes and wax crayons I'd assembled, including turmeric, ground red onion skins, and beet powder I'd made after dehydrating some of the last crop, so that my customers could experiment at home.

I'd gotten the herb starts under cover in time, thankfully, so I had plenty of fragrant lavender, rosemary, thyme, mint, and sage starts to line up at the front of my stall. I'd picked and bundled some larkspur bouquets from the storm survivors, arranging them in a galvanized bucket near the cash box, and, now that milking was back up to par, I had some rounds of fresh goat cheeses, several of which I'd decorated with fresh herbs and wildflowers.

As I arranged the candles behind the nests of soaps, I smiled to myself; next spring, with luck, I'd be selling candles made from my own golden beeswax, along with jars of honey produced on Dewberry Farm. I made a note to touch base with my friend Serafine; I'd ordered bees through her supplier, and I needed to set up my hives in the next few weeks; they would be here by the end of April. I also needed to finish tiling the backsplash in the kitchen, and find someone to put in the HVAC system for the little house down by the creek. And I still hadn't finished getting in the last of the tomatoes. Plus, I still hadn't found Cinnamon, and Dottie's abrupt departure and Eva's death were still bothering me. Were they connected?

And who had killed Eva?

I tried to push thoughts of Eva and Dottie and all my undone projects aside and brought myself back to the coolness of the spring morning, and the lovely purples and pinks of the larkspur bouquets. I was going to be hosting a dyeing workshop in the community tent in about thirty minutes, and had arranged for Molly's daughter Brittany to watch my stall while I set everything up. I had just finished arranging the last of the dyed eggs when she turned up.

"Hey, Brittany!" I said. "Ready for your shift?"

"I think so," she said.

I ran through the credit card payment process with her one more time, just to be sure. "The prices are all marked, and here's a calculator if you need help with numbers. Just record the sales in this notebook, and I'll be back in an hour."

"Will do," she said. "Good luck with the egg-dyeing workshop!"

"Thanks!" I said as I gathered my supplies and headed over to the area of the Town Square that had been designated for workshops.

The tables, thankfully, were covered with plastic tablecloths. I'd made dye ahead of time and stored it in plastic milk jugs, and boiled several dozen eggs. I set up several dyeing stations, along with wax crayons, dippers, and small cups of dye. I'd barely finished when a phalanx of families arrived, followed by a contingent from Sunset Home... including Dottie, who was looking a bit shell-shocked in her wheelchair.

I explained the process, demonstrating the beautiful yellows and pinks you could get from turmeric and beets, and then got everyone started dyeing eggs. As everyone got busy dunking their eggs, I walked over to my former neighbor, who was staring blankly at the courthouse while the woman next to her maneuvered an egg into a cup of turmeric dye.

"Are you doing okay?" I asked.

"I'm holding up," she said dully. There was no sign of the sparkle I was used to seeing in her eyes.

"I'm sorry I didn't get to say goodbye, by the way. I had no idea you had moved until I saw the 'For Sale' sign."

Dottie blinked at me. "The what?"

"The 'For Sale' sign," I repeated. "Faith Zapalac was putting it up when I got home yesterday."

She paled. "He told me he wasn't going to sell it just yet. We were going to try out the home, see what I thought."

"Well, then, just tell Faith you're not ready to sell yet."

"I... I don't know if I can," she said. "There were some court things, and... well, he's managing everything for me now."

"Court things?" I asked, feeling a pain in the pit of my stomach. "What kind of court things?"

"He said it was all just too much for me to manage." Her voice was wobbly. "He told me he'd take care of me."

As she spoke, an efficient-looking woman marched over to me. "Are you upsetting her?" she demanded.

"I don't mean to," I said. "She's my neighbor. Her house went up for sale yesterday; she didn't know it was going to be sold."

"We're taking good care of her at Sunset Home," the woman said briskly. "We take care of all our residents. Now, then, Dorothy, aren't you going to dye some eggs?"

"It's Dottie," I said. "Or Ms. Kreische."

The woman pursed her lips, and I caught a flash of irritation. "It'll be fun," she insisted.

"I don't think so. I... I don't feel very well," Dottie said. "Can I go back to the home?"

"I'm afraid not," the woman said cheerfully. "The outing lasts until two. You'll be just fine."

"I need to call my son," Dottie said.

"We can do that when we get back," the woman replied. "Now, then. Why don't you dye an egg like your friend, here?"

'She's not my friend," Dottie said shortly; I could see just a glimmer of her former spark. "I just met her on the bus."

"Well, I'm sure you'll be friends soon enough. I have to go check on everyone else, but you should be dyeing eggs," the caretaker said sternly, giving me a nasty look before she bustled off to help a man whose egg had ended up in the grass.

"You can use my phone," I told Dottie quietly.

"I know my son's number by heart."

I unlocked my phone and handed it to her. She dialed it with shaking fingers, then held it to her ear. "Jessie, this is your mother. I... I heard the house is up for sale. I'm sure there must be some mistake. Can you call me, please, or come by?" She paused, and added, "I love you. Give the kids a hug for me," and hung up, looking forlorn.

I put a hand on her bony shoulder.

"What do I do?" she whispered.

"Talk to him," I said. "What kind of 'court stuff' did he do?"

"He's taken over my finances for me," she said.

"Do you mean he has power of attorney?" I asked.

"I think it's something different," she said. "I'm not sure."

"Does Jennifer know what's going on?"

"I don't think so," she said, shaking her head. "He told me not to mention it to her."

"I think it might be time to talk to her," I suggested.

She ducked her head. "She'll be mad at me."

I didn't respond to that. "Do you have her number?" I asked.

She nodded. "But I don't want to call her now. I'll do it when I'm back at the home."

At that moment, the caretaker bustled back up. "I'll take care of Dorothy," she informed me.

"Dottie," I corrected her again.

"Dottie," she said. "Time to say goodbye. Let's go!" she said, turning Dottie's chair around before she had a chance to say anything else.

I watched her go, feeling a sense of foreboding. What "court stuff" had her son put into place?

And if Dottie didn't want to sell her house, why was it on the market?

∼

I STOPPED at the Blue Onion stall on my way back from the dyeing workshop. Quinn had set up a festive booth decorated with Easter bunnies and chicks. Even better was the array of fresh hot cross buns, maple twists, glossy rounds of homemade bread, pans of cinnamon rolls, and a variety of sandwiches and salads to go. I found myself transfixed by a cinnamon roll, and realized suddenly that it had been quite a while since breakfast.

"Um... can I help you?" Quinn asked with a grin.

"I'll take six of each," I said.

She laughed. "How about a sandwich and a mazanec to go?"

"A what?"

"Czech Easter bread. It's my grandmother's recipe."

"I'm game," I said. "Those grandmothers really knew what they were doing in the kitchen, didn't they?"

"We're none too shabby ourselves," she reminded me. "How did your workshop go?"

"It went well, except for Dottie," I told her, and relayed what Dottie had said about her son having legal rights.

"So her son put the house on the market?"

"Apparently."

"What kind of leverage does he have?"

"That's what I'm wondering."

"I know you mentioned Dottie talking about maybe selling the farm before the tornado, but Jennifer didn't say anything about it or her brother taking things over when she was here. I'm going to give her a call after the Market."

"I hope everything's okay," she said.

"So do I," I said, but I knew that everything wasn't. Not at all.

10

"What's wrong?" Brittany asked when I got back to the stall.

"Is it that obvious?" I asked.

She grinned. "You're like my mom. You always get a groove between your eyebrows when you're worried. Did the workshop not go all right?"

"No, it went well, in fact. I sold about fifteen dyeing packets."

"I sold about five here while you were gone," she said. "The egg soaps are popular, too."

"I'm glad they're selling," I told her. "I was a little bit worried I'd be stuck with several egg cartons of soap."

"So if the workshop went well, what's wrong?"

"I'm just worried about my neighbor, is all. I have a few things I need to check out."

"Like Mom's worried about Ethan," she said. "Speaking of which, she wants you to come to dinner soon."

"I'd love to!" I said. "When?"

"I don't know, but soon," she said. "I'll tell her to call you.

She's hoping you can help her figure out what to do with Ethan, I'm guessing."

"I've heard things have been tough," I told her. "Between you and me, do you have any insight into what's going on with him?"

"I don't know," she said. "He used to tell me things, but recently, he's kind of clammed up. I'm worried about him, though."

"Why?"

"Well, I guess Mom told you she caught him smoking. And I found a whiskey bottle in the back of the barn a couple of days ago."

"Does your dad drink whiskey?"

She shook her head. "I don't know if I should tell Mom, or if it's just going to stress her out more."

"I think you should probably show her," I said. "What do you think is causing all the trouble?"

"You know Ethan's never been superpopular at school," she said. "When a new neighbor and his daughter moved in down the road, Ethan started spending a lot of time over there, and he... well, he changed."

"What do you know about them?"

"Not a whole lot," she said. "I know June's dad works at the wool shop part-time."

"Wait. Her dad is Edward Bartsch?"

She nodded. "He's an artist, Ethan told me. I think he wants to be like him when he grows up. I saw some of his painted eggs for sale over at the wool shop stall; they look pretty good." She paused. "Do you think maybe that's why Ethan is hanging out with June so much? Because of her dad?"

"It's a possibility," I said. "Do you know what he's up to when he sneaks out at night?"

She shook her head. "I tried to catch him once, but I fell asleep." She cocked her head. "He did come back with some white stuff on his jeans the other day."

"White stuff?"

"Yeah," she said. "He was doing his own laundry, which I kind of thought was weird. When I went to ask him why, he shoved it into the washer fast, but not before I noticed it."

"Did you ask him about it?"

"Not yet," she said. "It wasn't the time, if you know what I mean. He was in a mood."

"Tell your mom," I suggested.

"I will," she promised. "In the meantime, if it's okay with you, I'm supposed to meet a few friends. Is it all right if I go?"

"Of course," I said. "Thanks so much for your help." I paid her for her time and sent her off, then turned as the mayor walked up to the booth. She wore jeans and a cowboy hat, as was her habit, and picked up one of my soaps in a weathered hand.

"These smell good, but I sure would hate to mess 'em up by using them!" she said, sniffing one of the pale purple lavender egg soaps.

"You can always tuck them into a drawer," I suggested. "Or leave them out, like potpourri."

"Not much of a potpourri type of gal, but I might do the drawer thing." She rolled the soap around in her palm for a moment, then looked up at me with sharp blue eyes. "How are things at the farm? I hear you got hit by the tornado."

"I did," I said. "The house is okay, but the little house and my garden took a hit, and I'm still missing one of Carrot's kids... Cinnamon."

"Insurance taking care of you okay?"

"I don't know yet." I'd called, but hadn't heard back from the adjustor. "How's your mom doing?"

Mayor Niedermeyer grimaced, still rolling the soap around in her hand. "She's not so hot. She misses Eva... I do, too. That woman was a godsend; I've never seen my mother happier. Eva was a big help to her."

"I'm so sorry," I said.

"You found her, didn't you?" she asked. "Down by the creek."

"I did," I confirmed.

"There are a lot of sad people, and I don't mind sayin' I'm one of them," the mayor said. "She touched a lot of lives."

"That's what I'm hearing. I just can't figure out who would have killed her."

"She must have made an enemy somewhere down the line," Mayor Niedermeyer said. "I don't know who, though; and usually, in a town like this, word travels pretty fast."

"Dottie said something about Eva having boyfriend problems... did she ever say anything to you or your mother about that?"

"Not to my knowledge," she replied, looking thoughtful. "She did have a beef with Sunset Home, though. Talked about 'those poor people in the home' all the time. That was really the only issue Eva and I had... now Mother's taken that right off the table as an option."

"I heard Eva got fired from there a while back," I said.

"She did," the mayor said. "I heard an earful about that, I'll tell you. Said they weren't taking good enough care of the folks who lived there. She wanted me to go to bat for her, but I wasn't sure how I could help."

"Did she say why she was fired?"

"She said it was for caring too much," the mayor said. "I called to check up; she treated the patients well. They said it was just a personality conflict. Word is she had some issues with one of the directors at the home."

"What kind of issues?"

"I think she thought some of the residents were being neglected. That they were simply 'cash cows,' as she put it. And I heard a lot about some woman named Jerri."

"Jerri?"

"Yeah. She was talking big about some kind of lawsuit. I don't think anything ever came of it, though."

I glanced over to where the woman from Sunset Home was herding her charges, over near Gus Holz's stand. And then I started wondering about Gus. Since he'd started dating Flora, he'd begun painting his birdhouses a variety of rather bright colors. I suspected Flora had had a hand in that, and I was curious if they were selling.

I was also curious about what he and Eva had been doing dining in La Grange.

I turned back to the mayor. "Dottie mentioned something about Eva having multiple boyfriends," I said. "Did she ever mention who she was seeing?"

"Last we talked, she was spending a lot of time with that artist fella who moved to town not long ago... the one who works at Buttercup Weavers and Knitters."

"That's what I heard, too," I said. "Did she ever say anything about anyone else?"

"Not that she told me. She seemed excited about him," the mayor said. "That's the only one she ever talked about. But now that you mention it, she did seem... distracted during her last days."

"Distracted?"

"Just not her normal self. Preoccupied. Leaving the kettle on the stove too long, burnin' the toast..."

"Did she say why?"

"Come to think of it, she did want to talk to me about

somethin'," she said. "We never did have a chance to chat, though... She caught me just as I was late for a meetin'. I told her we'd set something up, but it slipped my mind and she didn't bring it up again."

"When was this?" I asked.

"Last week sometime," she said. "Why? You lookin' into it?"

I shrugged. "I'm just wondering what happened to her. Plus, I'm worried about Dottie."

"I am too," the mayor said. "I had no idea she was fixin' to sell up and move to the home."

"I think it may be her son driving the decision," I said.

"Some days, it doesn't seem like a bad solution. I don't know what I'm gonna do now that Eva's gone." She sighed and adjusted her hat. "In the meantime, I'll get a few of these soaps for my mother. And maybe one of those cheeses for me? I like the rosemary."

"Of course," I said, and wrapped up her purchase. I felt a rush of satisfaction as I pulled one of the creamy white rounds decorated with sprigs of rosemary from the cooler; I'd gotten better at cheesemaking with practice, and my product not only tasted divine, but was pretty to look at, too. "If you get a chance to talk to your mother, could you ask her if she has any ideas about Eva?" I asked as I handed her a small bag.

"I will," she told me. "And thanks for these," she said. "I'm addicted to your goat cheese. If I don't cut back, I'm going to have to go up a jeans size."

I laughed. "Cheese is good for you. Just don't overload on maple twists and Easter Bread from the Blue Onion, and you'll be fine!"

"That mazanec is addictive, isn't it?"

"Weird name, but I hear it's yummy," I said. "I haven't tried it yet, but I've got a loaf of it tucked under the table for later."

"Lucky you," she said. "If I were you, I'd avoid that candy booth, too."

"I saw that," I said. "Those chocolate bunnies look exquisite."

"I had a sample. They taste even better than they look. She may be openin' a store in Buttercup, she said."

"Is there enough local business to support a fancy chocolate shop?"

"I know I'll be supporting her," the mayor said. "She gave me a sample of hot chocolate that was life-altering."

"I'll definitely have to check it out, then."

The mayor peeked into her bag and touched her hat. "Thank you for the cheese, ma'am. I'll let you know if Mother comes up with anything on Eva."

"Thanks," I said. "And let me know if anyone finds a homeless kid!"

The mayor's blue eyes twinkled. "Of the caprine variety, you mean?"

I laughed. "Definitely."

As she strolled toward the next booth, I spotted Gus trotting back to his birdhouse booth with one of Bubba Allen's barbecue sandwiches in a paper tray. It looked good; I might have to dart over and pick one up, myself. His brisket was melt-in-your-mouth tender.

"Gus!" I called. He turned, surprised, and his face broke into a smile when he saw me.

"Howdy, Lucy!"

"How're the new birdhouses selling?" I asked.

His smile dimmed a bit. "Not as well as I'd like, to be honest, but Flora wanted me to give it a shot, so..."

"I understand," I said. "Hey," I added, "did you hear about Eva?"

"Whole town heard about Eva," he said.

"Did you know her?" I asked.

His eyes darted away from me, and my stomach sank. "Not really," he said. "Anyhow, I'd best get back to my booth." He seemed in an awful hurry to get away all of a sudden.

"I'll stop by in a bit if I can get away," I said. "I hope you move some birdhouses!"

As he hurried away, a gaggle of Austin shoppers descended on the booth, oohing and aahing over the blown eggs and the herb starts. I gave out several samples of cheese, and spent the next two hours selling and wrapping my wares. I was down to the last three cheeses when Quinn stopped by the booth.

"Hey, are you around later on?" she asked.

"I'm headed home after the Market," I said. "Why?"

"I want to show you some of that stuff I found in the boxes from my mother's."

"That's right," I said. "I totally forgot."

"There's something weird about it though," she said. "I keep putting the box away, and it keeps on turning up in the middle of my closet."

"That is weird," I said, and again, I felt goosebumps rise on my arms. Out of the blue, what my grandmother had said in my dream—about mending things—or fixing things, popped into my head. There were too many odd things going on lately, if you asked me. Murders, old lockets, missing kids, boxes that moved themselves, strange dreams... I was ready for some normalcy.

"Come on over whenever," I said.

"Are you free for dinner? I could bring some leftovers from the cafe."

"That would be great," I said.
Quinn smiled. "See you soon, then!"

11

*B*rittany came back for the last hour of the market, and I took the opportunity to walk around a bit. The folks from Sunset Home had been loaded back into a bus and headed back to La Grange, and the traffic was starting to wind down. I took my time walking around the booths, checking out the wool shop's knitted egg aprons and Peter's produce booth, and then caught a whiff of the most divine chocolate scent I'd ever smelled.

It was coming from a booth swathed in spring-green cotton and filled with chocolate bunnies, chocolate eggs, and a big pot that smelled like what I imagined heaven must be like. The sign on the booth said "Chocolaterie Marta," and beneath it was a small woman with bright eyes and dark hair pulled up in a loose topknot. She wore a crisp blue apron and a bright, cheerful expression.

"What's in the pot?" I asked.

"Hot chocolate," she said. "Can I get you a cup?"

"Oh, yes," I said. It might not be brisk out, but I couldn't resist the scent. As she ladled up a cup for me, I introduced myself. "I'm Lucy Resnick," I told her. "I own a small farm here in town. I hear you're looking to set up shop."

"I'm Marta Fernandez," she said. "I am looking... if I can find a place to rent," she added as she handed me a cup of silky dark chocolate. I took a sip and groaned; it was thick and velvety and had the most intense chocolate flavor I'd ever tasted.

"This is amazing," I said. "What's in it?"

"Chocolate," she replied with an impish grin.

I laughed. "It sure isn't Hershey's." I took another sip. The stuff was heavenly.

"No, it's not. I make sure to use only the best chocolate, with around seventy percent cocoa, and I've played with the recipe to make it velvety."

"Whatever you're doing, it's amazing."

"I sometimes make it with cinnamon, too, the Mexican hot chocolate way... only thicker and richer."

"I'll bet that's good," I said, "but I kind of like the pure chocolate. Where did you learn to do all this?"

"I studied in Switzerland," she said as I took another sip. "I've added a bit of a regional twist; I've got dulce de leche truffles, some chocolate-dipped pralines... all kinds of locally inspired recipes."

"That sounds amazing."

"I'm really hoping I can get a shop set up here... and that people will come and buy good chocolate!"

As she spoke, three more people wandered up to the stall, drawn by the scent of chocolate. As I watched, she sold three more cups of chocolate, four chocolate Easter bunnies, and a bag of chocolate truffle eggs.

"It looks like you'll do just fine," I said. "Where are you thinking of setting up shop?"

"I've been trying to lease a space on the Square," she said.

"The problem is finding something I can afford. I'm staying in La Grange for now, but I'd rather settle down in Buttercup."

"Why Buttercup? Why not Houston or Austin?"

She grinned. "I'm tired of cities. Besides, my sister lives in La Grange, and I'd like to be close to my nieces and nephews."

"It sounds like you're a tight-knit family."

"We are," she said. "And the shop won't be my only source of income. I'm hoping I can get a good mail-order business going, and in theory, property here should be less expensive than in a city. Besides," she added, "Buttercup is just so much quainter than La Grange."

"I can't argue with that."

"I'm staying at my sister's place now, but I think we'll both be happier when I have my own digs. I'm looking at other towns nearby, too, but I'd really rather have my business here."

"I understand," I said. "I chose to live here, too. It's a wonderful community. How long has your sister been in La Grange?"

"About five years," she said. "She's got a good job, and the kids are happy in school there."

"What does she do?"

"She's a nurse. She used to work at Sunset Home, but she just started working at a rehab facility."

"Small world," I said. "A friend of mine just moved to Sunset Home yesterday."

Marta grimaced. "I hope she's got someone keeping an eye on her."

"What do you mean?"

"It's not a good place," Marta said grimly. "You should

talk to my sister Linda sometime. Although I'm not sure how much she'll be able to tell you."

I pulled one of my cards out of my pocket and gave it to her. She handed one of hers to me in return. "I'd love to talk with your sister about Sunset Home."

"Sure," she said. "She's actually here with the kids. They were giving out free samples a little while ago."

"Sounds like a family business," I said with a grin. "Are you all free after the Market?" I asked on impulse. "Maybe you and your sister could come over to my farm for a cup of tea."

"I'd love that!" she said.

I gave her directions and reached for a bag of chocolate eggs. "How much?" I asked.

"On the house!" she said with a big smile.

∽

I GOT BACK to the farm with far fewer wares than I'd left with; the Market had been good. So good that I hoped I'd have enough merchandise to get me through the end of the Market, in fact. I needed to make more goat cheese... but I also needed to finish planting transplants and see about fixing up the roof of the little house I was renovating. So much for the slower pace of life in the country, I thought to myself. There were days I wished I could clone myself.

I'd just finished unpacking the truck when a van came bumping up the driveway. Chuck barked as I shielded my eyes and squinted at it: sure enough, a sign bearing her business name, Chocolaterie Marta, was affixed to the side of the van. A moment later, Marta, a woman around her age I guessed must be her sister, and two girls tumbled out of the van. I stepped outside to greet them.

"This place is beautiful!" the woman with Marta said, her round face cracking into a sweet smile. "You must be Lucy," she said, extending a hand. "I'm Linda. These are my daughters. Marguerite and Zooey."

"Nice to meet you," I said to the two girls. The older had solemn eyes and held out her hand. I took it and shook it with a smile as the younger did a little dance, announcing that her name was Zooey.

"Can I invite you in for a glass of iced tea?"

"We'd love that," Marta said.

"Can we go look at the cows?" Zooey asked.

"Of course," I said. "There are goats, too. And I'll take you to see if there are any eggs in the chickens' nesting boxes in a few minutes."

"You have chickens?" Marguerite asked, her eyes wide.

"She has a thing for chickens," Linda told me.

"They're over there," I said, pointing toward the hen house. As the girls trotted off to the hen house, I invited the two women into my grandmother's yellow farmhouse.

"This place is amazing!" Marta said, looking around at the wood floors, the pine table, and the pie safe tucked into the corner. Bluebonnet-carpeted hills receded into the distance outside the windows, and two goldfinches were perched on the feeder hanging from a crape myrtle. I saw the house with new eyes, and felt a rush of gratitude that I was able to live in such beautiful surroundings.

"Thanks," I said, smiling at her.

"Are you glad you moved to Buttercup?" Marta asked as she and her sister sat down at the table and I poured three glasses of tea.

"I am," I said. "I've made some wonderful friends here, and as you can see, it's a beautiful place to live."

"Was that little house here when you got here?" Marta

asked, looking out to where the small building perched on a knoll just up from the creek.

"No," I said. "I got talked into moving it here last year; it needed a home and some renovation or it was going to fall apart. Once I get it fixed up, I'll rent it out on weekends."

"I'd love to live somewhere like this," Marta said.

"Maybe you can!" I said.

"Maybe," she said longingly. Linda peered through the windows to check on the girls, who were tucking grass stems through the wire of the chicken enclosure.

"Is it okay if they do that?" she asked.

"Yes," I said.

"This place is lovely," Linda said. "It's not far from La Grange, but it feels like another world."

"Thanks," I said, taking a sip of tea. "Marta tells me you used to work for Sunset Home."

"I did, but thank goodness I found another job," she said. "Marta said your neighbor went to live there recently."

"She did," I confirmed. "Did you know that another one of their former employees died?"

"What? Who?"

"Eva Clarke," I said.

"Eva?" Linda blanched. "What happened?"

"Someone killed her. Down by the creek."

She raised a hand to her mouth. "No. I can't believe it. She was so nice!"

"I know," I said. "I've been trying to figure out what happened to her. Did she run into trouble with anyone at the nursing home?"

"She had a run-in with one of the guardians," she said.

"Guardians?"

She nodded. "That was one of the reasons I got out of there. There's a woman named Jerri Roswell who's a court-appointed guardian of a lot of the residents. She never shows up to visit, and I don't think she does a good job taking care of her wards."

"In what way?"

"She gets paid for 'handling their estates,' but most of the people I saw there had their houses sold off and weren't seeing much of the money. She just walks in, takes them away from their homes, and deposits them in the nursing home. Eva thought it was wrong, and she spoke up to the administrator."

"And?"

"It didn't go well," Linda said with a grimace. "Apparently that's a big part of the home's business. From what I could see, they weren't going to go after Jerri... I did the math once, and I think she was responsible for thirty to forty percent of their business."

"How does she end up being guardian? Does she know the people who are her wards? Do they choose her?"

She shook her head. "Jerri started a business a few years back. Since then, from what I could see, she preyed on people who had assets, not much in the way of family, and enough dementia that she could get them declared incompetent. Then the court appointed her as guardian and she took over everything."

"How is that possible?"

"It's possible," she said. "One of my patients, Rose, woke up one day to Jerri at the door. By the end of the day, she was in the nursing home, with no say over anything. Her house was sold within the month, and all of her personal effects sold in an estate sale."

"That's horrible!"

"It is," she said. "Eva thought so, too. I think that's why she was fired."

"Eva was going to file a lawsuit or something, right?" Marta asked her sister.

"She talked about it," Linda said, "but I don't know if she ever did it."

"That kind of sounds like what happened to my next-door neighbor," I said. "Her son just came in and bundled her off to the home. Within twenty-four hours, there was a 'For Sale' sign on the property."

"The one next door?" Marta asked.

I nodded.

"It's under contract," Marta said.

My stomach dropped. "What?"

"Some lady in high heels was pinning the sign on it when we drove by," she said.

12

"They got a buyer fast, it looks like," Marta said.

"I can't believe it," I said. "I have got to get in touch with Dottie's daughter." I grabbed my phone and dialed Jennifer's number, then left an urgent message. "Call me anytime," I said before hanging up and turning to Marta and Linda.

"Jerri's not her guardian, is she?" Linda asked.

"No," I said. "I think her son has taken control of her finances. I talked with Dottie today; she didn't know the house was even on the market. And now it's sold."

To whom? I wondered. And what would happen to that little patch of restored prairie?

"I hope you can find a way to stop it," Linda said.

"I just want to make sure Dottie's wishes are being honored," I said. "I don't think she wanted to move. If Eva hadn't been murdered..."

"Do you think maybe her son did in the home health aide so that he could have an excuse to take over and move her out?" Marta asked, voicing the same thing I'd thought of on multiple occasions. "I don't know him, but it sounds like he stands to gain if he's in control of her finances."

I thought about Dottie's reaction when we brought up her son the day Eva died. Was he in town? Had he called Eva to meet? I wished we'd been able to find her phone. Was there any way to track down phone records? I wondered. I'd have to ask Deputy Shames.

"I've thought about that, too" I mused. "Why do you think she was fired?" I asked Linda.

"I think she was causing trouble by advocating for the patients."

"I'd heard that, too. That just seems wrong."

"It is," Linda concurred. "I feel so bad for those poor people, but with Jerri in charge of everything legally, there isn't much anyone else at the home could do. Once a resident is made a ward, they and their family pretty much lose all their rights."

"I wonder how that works?" I mused. I'd have to find out more about this guardianship. Was Eva killed for being a troublemaker? I wondered. Or was Dottie's theory about boyfriends the right one?

"What's that little house down there?" Linda asked, pointing out the window and recalling me from my thoughts.

"Oh, it's a little house I'm trying to get in shape to rent out."

"Like, permanently?" Marta asked.

"I was thinking of doing weekend rentals."

"I might be interested in taking it long-term if you'd consider it."

"If it were done, we could talk, but I still have a ways to go."

"Maybe in a few months, once I find a place to open my shop?"

"Maybe," I said. I hadn't thought about having someone on the farm permanently, but it was worth thinking about.

"I'll give you my cell number," she said. "If you decide to rent it full-time, I can write you a deposit check whenever you want."

"Let's get it habitable first before we talk about that," I suggested. "And get your business set up, okay?" I suggested.

She laughed. "You're probably right. I got carried away."

"Nothing wrong with enthusiasm," I said with a grin. I didn't know how I felt about having someone rent the house long-term, but if I did decide to do it, Marta would be a lovely neighbor to have.

∼

ONCE MARTA and Linda and her daughters left, I spent a few minutes online finding out about guardianship. It turned out Linda wasn't too far off about how it worked. Once someone was declared incompetent and made a "ward," their "guardian" had full legal rights to everything... including whether or not family—if there was any—can come to visit. Although most wards no longer had close family, I found several instances where a family discovered one of their members had been made the ward of a professional "guardian" only after it was too late to do anything about it.

There wasn't much to becoming one in Texas. You had to pass a criminal background check, apply for certification, take an exam, and you were in. If you could find well-to-do, lonely older adults without family to protect them, I could see it becoming a lucrative business opportunity.

Was that what Jerri was doing?

I was starting to worry more and more about Sunset Home. I was going to have to visit Dottie soon, and check the place out.

I would have done more, but farm chores awaited me. I closed up the laptop and headed out to put on my work boots; I was hoping to get most of the day's work done before Quinn showed up.

As I headed out to the field with a tray of vegetable starts, Chuck dawdling at my heels, I passed the clothesline and stopped short. There were gaps along the line; the clothespins were still clipped to the narrow rope, but the clothing was gone.

As Chuck sniffed the ground under the flapping laundry, I did a quick inventory and identified a pair of missing jeans and two button-down shirts, one of which was my favorite, a white cotton blouse sprinkled with cherry blossoms. I scanned the ground, wondering if they'd somehow blown away, but there was no sign of them. I put down the starts and gathered up the dry clothes, folding them and replacing them in the basket I'd left at the end of the line, then heading back to put the basket in the kitchen, just in case there was a laundry thief prowling around Buttercup.

The incident niggled at me as I finished feeding and milking the goats and cows. Unless two shirts and a pair of jeans had miraculously blown away, leaving everything else untouched and vanishing into thin air, someone had stolen some of my clothes. Why?

I was still stewing on my missing blouse and mulching the vegetable starts with compost when Quinn's truck bumped up the driveway. I wiped my hands on my jeans and waved, then used a pitchfork to toss on a few last bits of compost before heading back to the farmhouse.

"I hope you don't mind that I brought Pip," Quinn said as the black dog bounded out of the truck. He'd been small when we rescued him, but he was now leggy and coming up on seventy pounds. Chuck barked in greeting from behind the fence, and Pip ran to the gate to greet him.

"I'm glad you did," I said.

"How is everything looking?" Quinn asked as I opened the gate to let Pip in, then watched the two dogs greet each other joyfully.

"It's coming together," I said as she retrieved a cardboard box from the passenger seat of the truck. "But I think someone stole some of my clothes off the line."

"What?"

"I know," I said.

"Creepy," Quinn breathed, tucking a red curl behind her ear. "Would you mind grabbing the bag from the floor of the truck? I brought dinner."

"Of course... thanks so much for bringing food!" I said, holding open the gate for Quinn as she carried the box through, then grabbing the big bag from the floorboard of the truck. "What are we having?"

"Baked potato soup, salad, and fresh bread," she informed me, depositing the box on the table on the front porch.

"And you brought your magic box," I said.

"I did. I hope it stays where I put it this time, though."

"Me, too," I said as we walked into the house together.

I showed Quinn the damage to the coop—she was as mystified as I was—and we spent the next half hour trying to figure out what was going on in Buttercup as we enjoyed Quinn's fabulous soup. She'd brought a few cookies, too, making dinner a decadent and entirely nonlow-carb dining experience, but I wasn't complaining.

We gave the dogs, who had worn themselves out in the yard playing, the dregs of the soup, then cleaned up the kitchen and headed into the living room with cups of tea and Quinn's box.

"I'm worried about you, Lucy," she said. "I know you're against guns, but being out here all alone..."

"I know," I said.

"I don't want you to end up like Eva," she said.

"I'll lock my doors at night," I promised.

"Sure you don't want to come stay with me?"

"I don't want to leave the livestock unattended," I said. "I promise I'll call if I get into trouble. Now," I said, "let's look at that box you brought."

She reached for it, unfolding the top of it. "It's just some things from my mother's house," she said. She pulled out some black-and-white family photos. "I've been meaning to look through it, but I didn't have the heart. But when it fell on the floor, I figured it must be time."

"I get that," I told her as she leafed through the photos. I knew there were still some things in the attic of the farm I should go through; I just hadn't had the time.

"Look at this," Quinn said, pointing to one in which two women, hair pulled up in a Gibson-Girl style, stood in front of the Town Square. "Those are my great-great-aunts on my father's side," she said.

"They're pretty," I said. "The one on the left kind of looks like you; she's got a ringlet escaping."

"She kind of does, doesn't she?" Quinn said. "But there's one thing in this box that I can't understand."

"What is it?"

"This piece of fabric," she said, pulling out a tatty length of felted wool. "It looks like it was handmade."

"Hand-dyed, too, likely," I said, looking at the faded colors of mustard and gray.

"There's a piece of it missing," Quinn said. "In the corner."

"I see," I said. "It looks like someone stitched it up, though, so it wouldn't fall apart."

"Why would someone do that?"

"Maybe it got frayed and someone neatened it up?" I suggested.

"But the rest of it's in fairly good shape," Quinn pointed out, touching the fabric.

"It is," I said. "And it seems to have been made with a lot of care, too. It does seem weird that there's a corner missing."

"I know it's just a piece of fabric, but why is it in this box with all the family photos and the family Bible and everything?"

"I don't know," I said. "Any more luck on your grandmother's heritage, by the way?"

"Not really," she said, "but I know when she was born. Look at this," she said, pulling out an old, leather-bound book and opening it.

"It's in German!" I said.

"They must have brought it over from the old country," she said. "The publication date is in the 1800s."

She opened it up to the front page, where a list of names had been inked in multiple hands, in ink that was now fading. "Here's my grandmother's name: Elisabeth. She was born in October 1935, in La Grange."

"She was an only child," I said. "That must have been hard on a farming family. They relied on lots of children to keep things going."

"They weren't farmers, though," she said. "They owned the general store in town."

"What was their last name?"

"Zapp," she said.

"Oh! You never told me your family was connected with the Zapp Building!" The Zapp Building was now a hotel on the square. I'd always admired its decorative brick and its long, wavy glass windows, not to mention the barrels of colorful flowers the current owner kept blooming on the sidewalk outside.

"They sold it a long time ago," she said. "They ran the hotel for about thirty years, until it just got to be too much for them." She looked at the small list of names in the Bible. "Nobody had many children," she said. "Unusual for the time. I had some cousins on my father's side, but they moved to Pennsylvania and we've lost touch. My mother was an only child, so no family on that side."

"No wonder you're curious about your grandmother," I said.

"I just feel like there's something I'm missing," she said. "I've thought about it on and off over the years—and I did that DNA test a few months ago—but ever since the storm, it's just... it feels like I have to figure it out, you know?"

"I've had things like that," I said. "Maybe Ancestry.com will help."

"Maybe," she said doubtfully, fingering the soft cloth. "I don't know," she said. "I feel like there's a reason someone put this in here. And I'm never going to know what it is."

"You never know," I said, trying to be hopeful, although I was pretty sure she was right.

∼

We finally closed up the box, after admiring all the old photos and trying to imagine what Buttercup must have been like one hundred years ago, and returned to the kitchen for tea and a few more cookies.

"No word on Cinnamon, I presume?"

"None yet," I said. "And nothing on Eva, either."

"Have you talked with the guy she was seeing? Edward?"

"Not yet," I said. "I should probably stop by with some brownies or something. Besides, I want to meet his daughter; apparently, Molly's son Ethan has been spending a lot of time with her, sneaking out at night and possibly getting into trouble."

"That doesn't sound good."

"I know," I said. "I hope they're not getting into too much trouble."

"You definitely need to go and be neighborly," Quinn said. "Which reminds me, I found the best brownie recipe ever the other day. Maybe you should make a double batch." She pulled it up on her phone. "How are you for milk chocolate chips?"

I checked the pantry. "I've got two bags of them."

"Let's get started then," she said, and started digging through my cabinet for pans. As she dug, Chuck and Pip stalked to the back door and began to growl. Goose bumps rose on my arms. Was my chicken coop vandal back? I turned on the back light and peered out into the darkening evening.

"What is it?" Quinn asked, joining me at the window.

"I don't know," I said. "I don't see anything, but the dogs are spooked."

We stared out the window for a long time, as the dogs growled and barked at our feet. Finally, they relaxed, and Quinn and I looked at each other.

"Wonder what that was all about?" she asked.

"I have no idea," I said, feeling uneasy. "Hopefully nothing. I think we would have seen it if someone was out there, don't you?"

"I think so," she said. "After that, I really need chocolate. Let's get these brownies made."

∼

THE SKY outside the windows had turned dark, the sky spangled with stars, and we'd just finished off our fourth brownie each when Quinn patted her stomach and said, "I need to move. I know it's late, but show me what you did today.

"You mean the vegetables?" I asked.

"Yes," she said. "I need to get outside and move a little bit."

"I have mixed feelings about it, honestly, but the dogs seem okay."

"They'd tell us if someone was here, and they've been quiet for over an hour," she pointed out. "Besides, this is Buttercup. We're not in downtown Houston."

"You're right about the dogs," I reflected. "It's probably just nerves; I'm still recovering from finding Eva. But I'm bringing my shovel, just in case."

We put our boots on and headed out the kitchen door into the cool spring night air. I did grab the shovel I'd leaned up against the side of the house while Quinn took charge of the flashlight. "You hardly need it, really," she said. "The moon's almost full."

"Let's take it just in case," I said.

"You're really nervous, aren't you?" Quinn asked. "That chicken coop incident got to you."

"It did," I admitted as I opened the back gate, the dogs at our heels. They both relieved themselves on Chuck's favorite rose bush—poor thing—and then followed us out into the field. They did seem unconcerned. Quinn was probably right; I was just jumpy.

"You made a lot of progress," she said, pointing to the neat row of broccoli starts I'd put in that afternoon. I'd spent a little bit on lettuce starts and reseeded the rest, hoping that if I rigged some shade cover over them once it started to get warm, I'd get a decent harvest before the heat of summer kicked in. "And you got the tomatoes in, too," she said, pointing to the row of new cages I'd bought and plunged into the ground. "And you got a scarecrow, too! That should help with the birds."

"I didn't put up a scarecrow," I said. "What are you talking about?"

"There," she said, flicking on the flashlight and pointing.

A rude scarecrow stood at the end of the second row, its mouth a red slash, its eyes black holes in white fabric. Below the crudely rendered face, my cherry blossom shirt bulged with straw, and my jeans sagged beneath it.

"I didn't put that there," I breathed.

"I should hope not," Quinn said, focusing the light on the hilt of the knife protruding from the chest of my favorite blouse. I gripped the shovel harder. "Somebody's got it in for you, Lucy," my friend said in a low, grim voice.

13

We took pictures of the scarecrow from all angles and studied the turned-up dirt for evidence.

"Footprints," Quinn said, pointing to divots in the ground leading up to and away from the awful scarecrow.

"Boots, it looks like," I said. The prints weren't huge, but they weren't tiny, either.

"Likely a man?"

"Or a woman with large-ish feet," I replied. I took a few photos of the prints, too, as Quinn and I followed them to the end of the row. Unfortunately, any further prints were lost in the long grass.

"Think they came through the gate?" Quinn asked.

"Probably," I said. We walked to both gates, but there was no further sign of boot prints in the moist ground.

"Maybe they just materialized out of nowhere," Quinn suggested. "Whoever it was sure didn't cross the creek, I'm guessing." Dewberry Creek was still swollen and rushing from the recent rains as we walked across the fence line back toward the farmhouse. We'd only gone about ten yards when we found two pieces of barbed wire lying on the ground. Someone had snipped through the fence between my land and Dottie's. Quinn frowned as she shone the light on the wire. "Well, this explains why we didn't hear any cars on the driveway."

"Glad we found this now," I said. "Otherwise Blossom would be through this like a shot tomorrow."

"Not to mention the goats," Quinn said.

I sighed; it was one thing after another lately. "I'll fix it in the morning, when it's light."

"Are you sure you don't want to come and stay in town with me?" Quinn asked.

I shook my head. "Thanks, but I want to make sure my animals are okay."

"That scarecrow was dressed in your clothing," she reminded me. "That was a threat."

"I know," I said.

"Who did it?" she asked.

"Someone who doesn't want me asking questions about Eva?" I guessed. "I don't know."

"I don't like you staying here alone," she said. "I've decided I'm bunking with you for the night. I've got Pip with me, so there's no need to go back into town."

"Are you sure?" I asked.

"I'm guaranteed fresh eggs in the morning, at least," she said. "Plus, I brought Mazanec."

"Provided our vandal doesn't come back," I said gloomily.

"You padlocked the coop, right?" she asked. "I'm sure it'll be fine."

I just hoped she was right.

∾

The rest of the night passed without incident, fortunately. Quinn and I shared omelets and Mazanec for breakfast, still speculating on who had put up that horrible scarecrow. "What's your plan for the day?" she asked finally as she washed the omelet pan.

"I thought I'd swing by Edward's house and see what he knows about Eva," I said. "I'll bring what's left of the brownies."

"Let me know how it goes," she said, then fixed me with a stern look. "And be careful. If you won't buy a shotgun, maybe you should take karate class with me sometimes. It's good to know."

"I'll think about it," I said. Quinn was well on her way to a black belt, I knew, her martial arts journey inspired by a violent ex. It might be nice to know how to defend myself, I thought. My eyes drifted out to where the scarecrow had stood the night before, and I suppressed a shiver.

Once Quinn headed to the Blue Onion, I called Opal at the station to tell her what had happened and sent an e-mail with pictures attached, then spent the balance of the day fixing the fence, putting in more vegetable starts, and checking on my animals (there was still no sign of the missing kid, alas). Once my outdoor tasks were done, I busied myself making a batch of cheese and then blowing a few more eggs and dyeing them; my market stock was running low. It was almost five before I finished my tasks and grabbed the plate of brownies from the kitchen counter.

As I drove past Dottie's farm on the way to Edward's house, I realized I hadn't connected with Dottie's daughter yet. I dialed her number again, hoping she would answer. This time, she picked up after the third ring.

"Jennifer? It's Lucy Resnick."

"Oh, Lucy," she said. "I saw you'd called, but I've been so busy I haven't had a chance to call you back. Thanks again for taking care of Mom during that tornado. Without you and Quinn... I don't like to think what might have happened."

"Well," I said, "I'm afraid I may have some bad news for you."

I could hear the fear in her voice. "Is Mom okay?"

"Healthwise, she hasn't changed. But did you know she's living in Sunset Home in La Grange and that the house is under contract?"

There was a stunned silence. Finally, she said, "What? You're joking, right?"

"I'm afraid not," I said. "I'm not a hundred percent sure, but I think it's your brother's doing. He moved her over there right away. I ran into him having lunch with Faith Zapalac down at the Blue Onion; almost immediately after, there was a For Sale sign on the property, and in almost no time at all, it says it's under contract."

"That jerk," she fumed, shock giving way to anger. "He's been pushing her for years. I've told him to back off, but he must have convinced her. Damn it all," she said, then apologized. "I'm sorry. I don't usually cuss, but..."

"I understand," I said.

"That's the house I grew up in! My children visit her there every summer! How could he do such a thing?"

"I don't know the situation, but I'd get in touch with your mom and find out what you can as soon as possible. I know there's an option period on contracts... maybe there's time for her to back out of it?"

"I'm heading up there right now," Jennifer said. "Thanks for telling me."

"Let me know if I can help," I offered.

"I might need help killing my brother," she said, then added, "I'm just kidding. Thanks for the offer."

"I get it," I said. I hung up a moment later, feeling sad for Dottie, and as I turned onto the road to Edward's place, found myself hoping Jennifer could find a way to keep the house in the family.

Edward lived in a house not too far from central Buttercup, about a half mile down the road from the Kramers'. It was a small farmhouse not far off the main road, surrounded by several old oaks and a few pear trees with nascent fruit. I pulled up behind an old yellow truck, grabbed the plate of brownies I'd made, and headed to the front door, hoping he would be home.

A girl around Ethan's age answered the door, her hair scraped back into a ponytail and her hands covered in paint. "Hi," I said. "You must be June. Is your dad here?"

She gave a brief shrug, then turned, took a deep breath and yelled "Dad!" at the top of her lungs. Her powers of projection were impressive; I almost dropped the plate of brownies.

"I'm coming," he answered from somewhere in the house. A moment later, he appeared, his hands covered in clay. "Oh. Hi," he said, looking surprised to see me.

"Lucy Resnick," I said. "We've run into each other before. I was neighbors with Dottie, and I knew Eva."

He nodded and turned to his daughter. "I've got it, June Bug."

She looked at me for a long moment and then disappeared back into the house. Edward's eyes dropped to the plate of brownies. "What are those for?"

"I figured it might be rough, with Eva gone," I said quietly. "I thought I'd bring a little something."

"Come in," he said, stepping back and letting me into the

house. "I've been working on some paintings in my studio," he said.

"I heard you were an artist. I saw some of your eggs at the market; they're amazing."

"I do all kinds of things," he told me. "I should probably just stick to one thing, but I think I'd be bored. I may open a full booth at the Market this summer," he said as I followed him into the room he used as his studio. "I've been playing with oils this winter, doing landscapes."

"They're beautiful," I said, looking at the rich colors on the canvases lined up under the window. I recognized many of the scenes, but in Edward's hands, the rolling hills took on new contours and depth. "You really are talented."

"I've got a decent eye," he admitted. "I don't know how long I'll have a job at the knitting shop, so I'm trying to find a way to make a living. Marketing art can be a challenge."

"Maybe, but you obviously know what you're doing," I said, admiring a large landscape on canvas depicting an incoming storm, a small barn huddled in the forefront of the frame. I thought of the tornado, and shivered. "Where did you learn how to do that?"

"I got an MFA at UT a few years back. It's hard to find a job as an artist, though. Unless you're a graphic designer, that is. I did a little of that, but I prefer working with my hands."

"Where do you want these?" I asked, lifting the plate of brownies as he picked up a paintbrush and made a minor adjustment on his work in progress, a landscape that looked rather like Dottie's farm, now that I looked at it.

"On the shelf is good," he said. "I could go for a snack, but I'm going to finish this first. Why don't you go ahead and have one?"

"Thanks," I said, lifting the plastic wrap.

"Let me just get this last bit done and I'll join you," he said. As he made a few adjustments to the little farmhouse, I set the brownies on one of the few clear spots on the bookshelf and sat down on a wooden chair across from him.

"Is that Dottie's house?"

He nodded. "I took a picture of it about a month ago," he said, showing me the printed picture he was working from. Although it resembled the painting taking shape on the canvas, it didn't have anywhere near the depth and beauty. Nor did it have the white and black SUVs in the driveway. I didn't recall seeing either of them at her house before. Whose could they have been? I wondered.

"Did you spend much time over at Dottie's?"

"I took Eva lunch a few times," he said, "and visited with Dottie a bit, but no, I didn't."

"Do you recognize these SUVs?" I asked.

"One of them could be her son's, but it's hard to see in the photo. And I wasn't usually paying attention to the vehicles in the driveway when I was there," he added.

"I'm so sorry about Eva," I said.

His face darkened. "I'm not just sorry," he said. "I'm heartbroken."

"You two were serious?"

He sighed. "We'd been seeing each other for almost six months, and I'd never known anyone like her. She was such a sweet, kind soul... she didn't deserve what happened to her." He looked up at me, and his eyes were angry. "I'll tell you what. I'm going to get the guy who did that to her."

A shiver went down my spine. There was a coldness in his voice that scared me a little bit. "Do you think you know who it was?"

"It's obvious, isn't it?" he said. "Dottie's self-absorbed son Jessie. He's been pushing Dottie to give him control of her finances for all this time, and Eva was telling Dottie not to do it."

"So you think it was Jessie."

"Who else could it have been? Eva dies, and the next day Dottie's in the home and the house is on the market." He jabbed angrily at the canvas, smearing the carefully applied paint, then swore under his breath and hurled the paintbrush across his studio. "I can't work. I'm too angry." As I sat quietly, he washed his hands, dried them roughly with a towel, and jammed a brownie into his mouth.

The air in the studio had the heaviness and threat of a building storm, and all I wanted to do was get back in my truck. I still had questions, though. "Did you talk to the police about your suspicions?" I asked when he had finished a second brownie and his breathing had slowed a bit.

"I did, but it's pointless," he said. "I'm an outsider. Rooster's known him for decades. He'll never believe me."

"Deputy Shames might," I suggested.

"She might, but with that numbskull Rooster running the show, what would it matter?" he asked.

Unfortunately, I had to admit he had a point. "Did Jessie ever threaten Eva?" I asked.

He nodded. "She was getting nasty notes. And phone calls, late at night. They were anonymous, of course, but I'm sure it was him; it got so bad she was afraid to be in her house alone."

"That sounds horrible," I said. "Did she report them the police?"

"She did," he said. "Rooster ignored her, of course. And now this." He swiped at his eyes. "She wanted me to stay with her, but I couldn't leave June here alone every night." He grimaced. "She'd told me the day before that she was scared, but I never thought anything would happen to her at work. I should have been there."

"Who was she afraid of?"

He darted a glance at me. "I'm not sure," he said, but I wasn't convinced.

"Who do you think was sending the notes?"

"Let's just say some people didn't appreciate the level of care she provided her clients."

That didn't tell me who had threatened her, but it did narrow it down. "Was it someone from the nursing home?" I asked.

His lips tightened. "That was a real three-ring circus, too," he said. "She told me all about it; that place was a racket."

"Why?"

"It was all about the money at that place. Eva told me all she wanted was for her clients to have a good quality of life, but the people who ran the place kept accusing her of 'interfering.' They treat those people like cattle." The muscles in his jaw worked. "I wish I'd been there to help her that day at Dottie's. I could have protected her."

"You couldn't be with her every minute of every day," I reminded him. "It's not like she was out walking alone at night."

"But what was she doing out there by the creek? That's not like her at all. She never would have left one of her clients like that, especially not with a storm coming."

"She didn't have her phone when we found her," I said, "but it wasn't in the house either. I wonder if someone called or texted her for a meeting?"

"A meeting out by the creek?"

"I don't know," I said. "I can't think why else she'd go out there." I took a deep breath. "Do you know if she might have been seeing anyone else?"

"No," he said, shaking his head vehemently. "It was just us." Tears leaked from the corners of his eyes. "After all the bad relationships, I finally find a good one, and now... now she's gone forever." He put his head between his hands and wept. I walked over to him and put a hand on his back. There was nothing I could do to make it better. All I could do was to be there for him as he grieved.

After a long moment, he swiped at his eyes again and sat up straight. "I need to get myself together."

"No, you don't," I told him gently. "Grief takes time."

"But I have to be there for June Bug," he said.

"That's true," I admitted. "But take it easy on yourself. It's a big loss."

"I guess you're right," he said. "But I have to find out what happened to her. And whoever killed her is going to pay the price."

As he spoke, June peeked around the doorway. I wondered how much she'd heard.

"Hey, June Bug," Edward said. "Lucy brought brownies. Want one?"

"Sure," she said, and took a small one from the edge of the plate.

"Nice to meet you," I told her. "How are you finding living in Buttercup?"

"It's okay," she said with a shrug.

"I hear you and Ethan Kramer hang out," I said.

Her face became guarded, and she shrugged. "We're just in the same English class," she said, and grabbed another brownie. "I've got homework," she said shortly, and vanished.

"What the heck was that all about?" Edward asked, looking puzzled.

I waited until I heard a door slam shut somewhere in the house before answering. "I don't know if you know, but there's a rumor that June and Ethan have been sneaking out at night together lately."

He blinked at me. "What?"

"I can't be one hundred percent sure, but that's what I've heard. Any idea what they might be up to?"

"No," he said blankly. "I guess I've been so caught up in my work and in Eva that I just assumed everything was okay with June." He glanced at the doorway she'd disappeared through a little while back. "What do you think they've been doing?" He blanched. "You don't think they..."

"I don't know," I said. "Ethan's sister Brittany said he came home covered in white stuff the other day. So maybe there's something else going on. But I know Ethan's mom is worried."

"I'm worried too," he said. "Sounds like it's time for a conversation."

I was glad he was taking it seriously. "Parenting sounds like so much fun," I said.

"It can be an absolute joy," he said. "I love June Bug more than I've ever loved anyone. But it's hard work. And you never know if you're doing the right thing." He grimaced. "I moved to Buttercup because she wasn't thriving in the suburbs, in that hypercompetitive school system, where everyone is on three soccer teams and cheerleading and drill team and all that. I thought she'd have a better chance of finding her tribe in a slower-paced town, but so far it hasn't worked out that way. And now, if she's getting into trouble..."

"We don't know what she's doing yet," I reassured him.

"I'm sure Molly would be more than happy to talk, so you can figure things out together."

"You think?"

"I'll check with her," I said.

He sighed. "Everything's just going south, isn't it? At first, Buttercup seemed like a dream come true. I met Eva, June seemed to be doing better... and now Eva's gone and June Bug's getting into who knows what?"

"Life is good at curve balls," I said, thinking of Dottie and the tornado and my missing kid, Cinnamon. "I guess we just have to do the best we can to handle them. I really am sorry about Eva, though."

"I'm sorry, too," he said. "And soon," he added in a tone of voice that made the hairs on the back of my neck stand up, "I won't be the only one who's sorry."

14

I had just finished milking Hot Lips when a truck bumped up the driveway. I smiled as I recognized it was Tobias's.

"What brings you here?" I asked as I walked over to meet him at the top of the drive.

"I missed you," he said, giving me a peck on the lips. "I know it's late notice, but I was wondering if you were up for dinner."

"That sounds terrific," I said. "I can whip up something here, or we can go out; whichever works for me!"

"I thought we'd head over to Bubba's Barbecue," he said. "I'm kind of in the mood for brisket."

"That sounds great," I said. "Let me just get cleaned up and we'll head over. We've got a lot to catch up on."

"We do?" he asked.

"You have no idea," I said, giving him a quick peck before going to get changed.

When I emerged from my bedroom a few minutes later, Tobias was in the rocking chair on the front porch with Chuck sprawled across his lap. Tobias patted my poodle's roundish tummy. "Looks like the diet dog food isn't doing the trick," he said.

"He's not a fan," I said. "I keep having to doctor it to get him to eat."

"What does 'doctor' mean?" Tobias asked. "Are we talking cucumber slices?"

"Not exactly," I admitted. "At any rate," I said, changing the subject, "how about that barbecue?"

"We'll have to talk about this more at your next vet appointment, young man," Tobias told Chuck in a stern voice, then gently put him on the floor and stood up. "Ready?"

"Absolutely," I said.

A few minutes later, we were headed across the rolling hills of Buttercup toward Bubba's, home of the best barbecue in Fayette County as far as I was concerned. The pecan pie was to die for, too. As we drove, I filled him in on the chicken coop vandalism and the creepy scarecrow.

"Did you report it?"

"I did," I said, "but I haven't heard back."

"I don't like it," he said. "Maybe you should stay with me for a few days."

"No," I said. "I don't want to leave the farm."

He sighed. "Any word on what happened to Eva?"

"No, but I had a disturbing conversation with Edward Bartsch," I told him. "He's convinced Dottie's son killed Eva."

Tobias gripped the steering wheel. "What? Why?"

"You know Dottie's place is already under contract, right?"

"Yeah. To a judge, from what I hear, under the auspices of some kind of real estate company."

"I'm not sure that's good news," I replied, wondering what was in store for Dottie's property. "At any rate, I got the feeling Edward thinks Eva was trying to talk Dottie out of giving Jessie power of attorney, or whatever she gave him to let him sell the house, and that he killed her to get her out of the way."

"Did he talk to Rooster about it?"

"He told me he did. He also told me it didn't go well."

"Big surprise there. What about the deputy?"

"I suggested that, too," I said. "I'm worried, though. And apparently his daughter June has been sneaking out with Ethan Kramer, and Edward didn't know anything about that."

"How do *you* know anything about that?"

"I heard it from Molly and her daughter Brittany," I said.

"All kinds of intrigue going on," he said. "Speaking of intrigue, I did get a call on a found kid..."

My heart surged. "You did?"

"Yes," he said, "but it wasn't Cinnamon. I'm so sorry, honey." He put a hand on my knee.

"She's probably gone, isn't she?" I asked sadly.

"I like to keep hope alive," he said, "but being away from her mother for so long... the odds aren't in her favor, unfortunately."

I sighed. "I know," I said. "I just wish I could have done something to prevent it. Maybe if I hadn't gone to Dottie's..."

"Going to help Dottie was the right thing to do," he reassured me. "You can't second-guess yourself. Things like this happen sometimes."

"I know," I said. "It's just so sad."

He patted my knee and gave it a sympathetic squeeze. We sat in silence, both lost in our thoughts, until he turned into the busy parking lot of Bubba's.

The brisket was tender and smoky as always, and I had to resist the urge to order a second plate, instead restricting myself to dessert. We'd just finished the last bit of pecan pie when my phone rang. It was Margaret Simmons, the owner of Buttercup Weavers and Knitters.

"You have to come down here right now..." She sounded frantic.

"What's wrong?" I asked.

"I don't know how to say this, but..."

"Just spit it out," I said.

"Okay. Okay." She took a deep breath that sounded like she might be hyperventilating. Finally, she said, "There's a dead man in my craft room."

15

"Wait," I said. "What?"

"In my craft room," she repeated. "There's a dead man."

"Who is it?" I asked, gripping the phone.

"I don't know," she said. "His face is... it's all green."

"Green?"

"Yes. I think someone..." she gulped. "Someone dyed him to death."

∼

Tobias and I got to Buttercup Weavers and Knitters before Rooster or any of his deputies. Margaret was sitting in the front room of the store, clutching a soft wool blanket and rocking back and forth, her face drained of color.

"Stay here," I told her as Tobias and I headed to the back. "We're just going to see if we can figure out who it is."

The man in question was, in fact, green. His face was stained with dye, as was most of his formerly plaid shirt, and he was lying in the middle of the craft room floor, trailing what looked like plant material from his thinning hair.

"Who is it?" Tobias asked.

I squinted at him; I was pretty sure I knew who it was, but with all the green dye, it was hard to be sure. Then I looked at the class ring glittering on the fourth finger of his right hand and my stomach sank. "I think it's Dottie's son Jessie," I said.

Tobias looked at me, his face grim. "Do you think Edward might have... you know?"

"I don't know," I said, but I felt sick. "Let's not mention that just yet, okay?"

"That could be considered obstructing an investigation," he pointed out.

"I said *yet*," I repeated.

"All right. If Rooster's track record weren't so bad, I'd object more. The question is, what is he doing in a knitting store?" Tobias asked. He glanced at his watch. "It's almost eight o'clock. Doesn't this place close at five?"

"Unless Margaret is hosting a workshop, it does," I confirmed.

"And why would he come to a yarn store? I don't want to stereotype, but he doesn't strike me as the fiber arts type."

"Maybe he was picking up something up for Dottie," I suggested. Although from what I knew of Jessie, running thoughtful errands wasn't something he often did for his mother. "Trying to ease the transition to the new place?"

"That seems more like something her daughter would do," Tobias said.

"I talked to her earlier today, incidentally" I said. "She was coming up to talk with her mother."

"Oh," Tobias said slowly. "And here is her brother. Dead."

"I suppose it's possible she was involved," I said. "But I don't want to jump to conclusions just yet. Besides, it's possible the same person killed both of them."

"Or it could be a revenge killing," Tobias said again. "If Jessie killed Eva, Edward might have decided to take justice into his own hands; I hate to keep saying it, but it's the obvious solution."

"Edward's strong, and killing someone this way would require physical strength," I pointed out. "It took some muscle to keep his head submerged."

"Assuming that's how he died," Tobias said. "We don't know if the dye job was just the icing on the cake, so to speak."

"I don't see any knife or bullet holes," I pointed out.

"No, but poison doesn't leave holes. I'd be curious to find out how he spent the day before coming here."

"And if his hands are green," I said. "That dye is pretty powerful, it seems."

"That's true." Tobias scanned the room, then touched the back pockets of Jessie's jeans. "Do you see a cell phone anywhere?" he asked.

"No." Just like Eva. Why were both phones missing? "Maybe Opal down at the station can round up some cell phone records."

"Be careful," Tobias warned me. "If you're going to investigate, please try not to broadcast it too loudly. I don't want you making yourself a target."

Deputy Shames appeared in the doorway. "Sorry to interrupt," she said. "You know this is a crime scene, right?"

"I know," I said, blushing.

"Why are you here, then?" she asked.

"Margaret called us," I said. "We came down to keep her

company."

"She's in the front room though," the deputy pointed out.

"We were looking to see if anything could be done," Tobias said.

She didn't look convinced. "Any idea who it is?"

"We think it's Dottie's son Jessie."

Her right eyebrow quirked up. "Being connected to Dottie seems to be a risky business, doesn't it?"

"Maybe it's just a coincidence," I suggested.

"Maybe. But I don't hold much with coincidence when it comes to crime."

Unfortunately, I had to admit I agreed with her.

∽

THE NEXT MORNING dawned bright and clear, with a quick rain shower that seemed to wash away all the darkness of the past few days and make everything fresh and clean. Unfortunately, however, things weren't that simple; two people were dead, and I still had no idea why. I spent the first few hours of the morning checking on my fledgling vegetables, feeding the chickens and collecting eggs, and doing my dairy chores. I kept a sharp eye out for any sign of Cinnamon, but I was starting to lose hope. As I finished milking the goats, finding some measure of peace in the rhythmic sound of the milk hitting the side of the pail, my thoughts turned to Eva and Jessie. Who would want to kill them both?

Did they both know something someone thought they shouldn't?

As I glanced over toward Dottie's land, another thought popped into my head. Now that Jessie was gone, could Dottie nullify the sale? I knew there was an option period;

could either the seller or the buyer choose to opt out? It wasn't exactly the best time to bring it up with Dottie, I knew, but if Jessie had sold her property against her will, I didn't have much choice.

I stroked Carrot, who had settled down since the loss of Cinnamon, but still wasn't quite herself. "I'm still looking," I assured her. I hadn't heard anything from the ad I'd put in the *Buttercup Zephyr*.

And speaking of missing, I kept thinking about those missing cell phones. Neither Eva nor Jessie had had theirs with them; I presumed the murderer had taken them. Why? And why kill both of them?

As I released Carrot to go rejoin Hot Lips and Gidget, I wondered if Deputy Shames had had any luck looking up phone records, or if she'd done it at all. I had a feeling both Eva and Jessie had gone to see someone, only to meet an untimely end. But who? The yarn store would point to Edward—and Eva was strangled with a knitted scarf—but why kill someone at your place of employment if you were looking to evade arrest? It didn't make sense.

I took a deep breath of cool spring air as I walked back to the farmhouse, trying to clear my mind. I had more cheese to make today, and I should probably dye a few more blown eggs for the Market, but despite my efforts, I found myself preoccupied with Eva and Jessie.

I had just finished putting the milk in the fridge and was washing my hands when my cell phone rang. I glanced at the number: it was Mandy Vargas from the *Zephyr*.

"Hey, Mandy," I said when I picked up.

"I hear you've been in the thick of things again," she said. "Two bodies this week?"

"Unfortunately, yes," I said.

"And I hear a local judge bought Dottie's land. He's using some company to do it, but it's him."

"What company?"

"Buttercup Holding Company," she said.

Something about the name sparked a response in me. Then I had a thought. "Can you look up what else that company's bought?"

"Sure," she said. "Why? You think it's related to what's going on?"

"I don't know. There's just something about it..." I looked over at the verdant pasture next door. "I think Dottie's son signed the contract; do you know if Dottie can back out of it?"

"I don't," she said, "but I'll see what I can find out. Can you give me any scoop on the two deaths? I understand Eva's was murder; I covered that yesterday. What about Jessie?"

"I don't think it was suicide," I said, "but I don't think I'm allowed to talk about it."

"Yarn store," she said. "I know Eva's boyfriend worked there. Love triangle, do you think?"

"I have no idea," I said.

"Well, let me know what you find out, when you can," she said. "By the way, I heard your place got hit by the storm."

"It did, but it could have been worse."

"That's when you found Eva, isn't it? During the storm?"

"It was," I said. "Hey... I think there may be something going on at Sunset Home in La Grange, by the way. Apparently, Eva was talking about reporting them to the police before she died."

"Sunset Home? I've heard of a few complaints about them, actually."

"The woman Eva tangled with there is named Jerri, apparently. I talked with another former worker, and she wasn't too pleased with the way the organization treated their residents. I'm going over to visit with Dottie shortly; I'll see if I hear anything, but if you could look into it on your end, that might help."

"Think it might have something to do with what happened to Eva and Jessie?"

"Both were connected to Dottie, and Dottie's now living at the place where Eva used to work... I don't know, but it seems like it might be worth checking out. Also... can you poke around and find out more about the sale? I'd go and ask Faith myself, but we aren't exactly fast friends."

"When did it go under contract again?"

"Just this week," I said. "Like I said, I think Jessie must have had power of attorney, because he shipped his mother off to Sunset Home and put the land up for sale the same day. It sold so fast it kind of makes me wonder if it wasn't arranged ahead of time."

"I'm on it," Mandy said. "Sure you don't have any extra details you can share about your discovery?"

"Sadly no," I said. "But if I do, I promise you'll be the first to know.

"You're still a reporter, aren't you? If you ever need a part-time job..."

"I'll think about it," I said, looking at the fridge full of unprocessed milk, "but to be honest, I kind of have my hands full already. And did you put that ad in? The missing kid ad?"

"It's running," she said.

"Thanks." I hung up feeling slightly better.

I made a quick call to the station, hoping I'd get Opal so I could mention phone records, but she wasn't in yet, so I said

I'd call back later. As I put down the phone, I thought again about the slip of paper I'd found in Eva's pockets: Cup Holding. Short for Buttercup Holding? If it was, I would be very curious to find out what Mandy found out about their recent activity... I was guessing that would get us one step closer to what had happened to Eva.

I just hoped it would be enough.

∽

Sunset Home was a severe-looking institution several blocks away from downtown La Grange. It was housed in a long, low-slung building constructed of concrete block painted a sullen beige. The only greenery interrupting the drab vista consisted of a few sprigs of grass poking up through cracks in the pavement. The building was dotted with small, high windows that reminded me of a minimum-security prison. Not that the view was spectacular—across the street were a self-storage facility and an auto parts store —but slightly bigger windows would have been at least a tad less depressing.

I pulled open the clouded-glass door and stepped into the reception area. The concrete floor was scuffed, and an unhappy-looking young woman at the front desk gave me a look that was at once bored and disapproving before her eyes flicked back to her monitor. A green vase full of bleached, dusty, fake daisies was the only nod to cheerfulness. I looked down at the vase of larkspur in my hand, thankful I'd stopped to pick some flowers. Sunset Home might be only a few miles away from Dewberry Farm, but it felt like an entirely different universe. A not-very-nice universe.

"Excuse me," I said. "I'm here to visit Dottie Kreische?"

"Do you have an appointment?" the young woman asked, her voice tinged with irritation. This time, she didn't look up from her monitor.

"No," I said. "I just wanted to stop by."

She gave a long sigh and tapped at her keyboard. "Down that hall to the left. Room 123."

"Thanks," I said, and pushed through two metal double doors into a fluorescent-lit corridor.

Dottie's room was about seven doors down on the left. I knocked, and when I heard a feeble "Come in," I opened it.

She lay in a bed in the middle of a small room, looking about ten years older than she had before moving. There were only a few tidbits of her former life with her; a handmade quilt covered her legs, a worn Bible sat on the table next to her, and a picture of Jessie was propped up on a shelf under the window. I set the larkspur down next to it; it added a little pop of color, but not nearly enough to make the room even remotely close to cheerful.

"Lucy," Dottie said, her voice dull. "My son. He's gone."

I walked over and sat down in the cracked vinyl chair next to the bed, taking her bony hand in mine. At the house, she was usually dressed when I saw her; today, she wore a pink dressing gown with a few stains around the collar. "I'm so, so sorry about Jessie," I said.

She gave me a slight nod, but her eyes filled with tears. "I just... I just can't believe it," she said. "My little boy."

I gave her hand a squeeze.

"And Eva. And my home. All gone, so fast. I can't... I can't take it all in."

"I know," I said. "It's a lot, and it's awful."

"I hate this place," she said dully.

"Maybe you don't have to stay here," I suggested.

She turned to me, her eyes hollow. "But my house is gone," she said. "Sold. Gone."

"It's under contract," I said, "but you haven't closed on it yet. Maybe there's still something we can do."

"But Jessie thought it was better for me financially to sell it. What if I can't stay? What if I can't afford it?"

"Let's see if we can stall the sale first," I said, "and find you a financial adviser to help figure out the situation."

"I... I just can't even think about it right now," she said. She looked like she was still in shock. I imagine she probably was.

Still, the clock was ticking. I didn't want to press her, but I didn't want her to run out of time—and options—either.

"I know this is a terrible question to ask," I said, "but do you have any idea who might have wanted to harm your son—or Eva?"

"No," she said. "To be honest, I thought... well, he was so angry at Eva, the thought crossed my mind that maybe something had happened between them. But now..." Her face crumpled. I reached for a tissue and handed it to her, wishing I could do something more to salve the obvious pain in her heart. "I've lost my baby," she said. "I just don't know if I have any reason to go on."

"What about your daughter?" I asked. "And your grandchildren?"

"I just... Jennifer and I never got along too well," she said. "She was always jealous of Jessie, I think. I tried, but I never knew how to fix things with her."

"I know it's hard to even think about it right now, but maybe that's something to work toward," I suggested. "I know she loves you."

"And I love her," Dottie said. "It's just... we've never seen eye to eye on things. She came to visit, but it didn't go well... she was really upset."

"How is it here, by the way? Do you like it?"

"It's horrible," she said in a whisper, but her face lost a little bit of the dead look. There are three women here who were turned out of their homes last month. Someone just swept in and took over everything."

"What?"

She nodded. "There's a woman who says she's the 'guardian' of all of them, but I think all she does is take over their assets and leave them here."

"What about their families?" I asked.

She shook her head. "None of them have children, and their husbands have died. Apparently the court or something decides they can't take care of themselves and then assigns someone to take over for them. And they have no say at all about anything. It's awful."

It didn't sound too different from what Dottie had experienced with her own son... and was in line with what Edward had told me. "Who is the guardian?"

"It's somebody named Jerri," she said. "No one sees much of her, though."

"I heard Eva was thinking about reporting someone to the police. Do you know anything about that?"

"She was on the phone a lot, but I don't know how much was about this place. I know she was upset about Jessie's plans for me," she said. "She and Jessie argued about it; they thought I couldn't hear, but I turned up my hearing aids. Jessie said it was because she didn't want to lose a client, but I know Eva cared for me. I would have kept the house, you know, but Jessie said I couldn't afford to." She sighed. "I loved Eva, but she stirred up a lot of trouble between the kids."

"How so?"

"Like I said, she wasn't on board with what Jessie wanted to do. Finally, I had to stop saying anything to anyone. Including Eva." She sighed again. "I know my son always wanted what was best for me. He's managed my finances for the last couple of years." Which evidently resulted in a fire sale of the house and Dottie being plunked down here, I thought to myself. Not someone I'd be quick to hand over my finances to, that was for sure.

"Maybe your daughter can help you figure things out," I suggested. "Find a way to get you back home."

"But Jessie said I couldn't afford it," she said, her face looking drawn and hopeless. She gave a feeble shrug. "Besides, it's too late."

"I'm looking into that," I told her. "But in the meantime, can you do me a favor?"

"I suppose so," she said. "What?"

"Can you find out more about that guardianship thing from the women you met?"

"Why?"

"I just... have a feeling," I said.

She sat up a little bit. "This couldn't be connected to what happened to my poor boy, could it?"

"I don't know anything yet," I said. Which was true. But I had my suspicions. And although it might not be linked to what had happened to Jessie, I had a hunch someone would be very interested in keeping Eva quiet about what was going on in the nursing home.

Maybe permanently.

"I just got a call about a stray kid," Tobias said when I

swung by the vet clinic on the way back to the farm. I'd been planning on seeing if he was up for lunch, but this was much more interesting news.

"You're talking goats, right?"

He grinned. "Right. I was just about to call you," he said. "Want to go check it out with me?"

"Of course!" I said. "Is she in okay shape?"

"She turned up last night," he said. "A little weak, but they've been bottle-feeding her, and she's taking the milk."

"Do you really think it could be Cinnamon?"

"That's what we're going to find out," he said as we climbed into his truck.

As we drove east, I filled him in on my visit with Dottie that morning. "I've got Mandy Vargas looking into the sale; I'm hoping she can tell me if there's anything we can do to stop it. Apparently Jessie said she couldn't afford to live in the house anymore, but I'll believe that when I see the balance sheet."

"Dottie always was frugal," Tobias said. "She takes good care of her stock, but she's not one to buy the latest things. I think some of those dresses she wears belonged to her mother."

"Not a bad way to be," I said, thinking of how my own purchasing habits had changed since moving to Buttercup. I used to have the latest gadgets—flat screen TVs, new phones, you name it—and at least twice a year I went shopping to update my work wardrobe with new shoes and clothes I really didn't need. Now, although I wore through my clothes a lot faster—being on your knees weeding is hard on jeans—I spent more of my time producing things than consuming them. I hadn't reflected on it before, but it was a satisfying change: not only for my bottom line, but for my quality of life.

Not that things were without trouble. I was still worried about my expenses after the recent storm... and hoping that the missing kid would turn out to be Thistle's lost sister.

As we drove, we passed an old barn with what appeared to be graffiti scrawled over the side of it. "Another hit. What do you think the words mean?" I said, trying to decipher the intricate letters.

"It's a feedlot protest, I think. They're popping up all over town," Tobias said. "Someone even graffitied a cow the other day."

"You're kidding me."

"Nope. They seem to be hitting the cattle ranches," he said. "One of the big ranches down the road from Peter's place got tagged a couple of days ago. A few of the ranchers think he's the one doing it."

"It's different from the graffiti at my place," I said. "And I don't have anything to do with feedlots."

"They don't seem to be connected," Tobias agreed.

"The idea that Peter is doing this is crazy, though. I know how he feels about feedlots," I said, "but I can't imagine him taking to painting signs on other people's barns. Besides, he's got enough on his hands at Green Haven right now; it's kind of the busy season."

"I know," Tobias said, "but you know how people get. Peter represents a new way of farming, and not everyone's comfortable with that. He's been pretty vocal about things, and a lot of folks don't like it."

"Change is hard for people," I said as the ranch with its decorated barn receded from view. "When did all this start?"

"About a month ago," he said. "The designs used to be simpler; now they're becoming more elaborate."

"It kind of looked like a stencil," I said.

"I thought so, too," he told me. "The first ones were just

spray paint scrawled across the side of barns. They're all signed, though."

"What's the signature?"

"SAAC," he said, grimacing.

"Mandy did a short article about it in the *Zephyr* a while back, but I haven't heard anything since. I don't think it's the same people who spray-painted my chicken coop, though."

"No," he agreed. "It doesn't fit the pattern."

I sighed. "I don't know who's doing it, but I worry they might get more than they bargained for one of these times."

"I hadn't thought about that, but you're right," I said. People in Texas took their right to defend their property with firearms seriously. I'd considered buying a gun a few years back, when Quinn's violent ex was stalking her, but had decided against it; I just didn't feel comfortable having one in the house. Although most folks used guns for snakes and coyotes—both of which I preferred to coexist with, since as far as I could tell, the critters got to Buttercup long before we humans did—many of my fellow farmers and ranchers wouldn't hesitate to defend their property from animals or humans. Which meant whoever was tagging barns was putting themselves at risk every time they decided to leave their mark. "What do you think SAAC stands for?" I mused.

"I have no idea."

"Not a great acronym if you don't know what it means."

"Maybe it's part of the mystery," he said as we turned into a gravel drive flanked by a limestone gate and tall fences. "Here we are," he said.

"It's kind of far away from Dewberry Farm," I said. "A long way for a kid to go."

"They can be surprising sometimes," he said. "And maybe the twister picked her up and moved her."

"Like Dorothy in *The Wizard of Oz*?" I asked. I was trying to keep my hopes up, but I was guessing I was going to be disappointed. "This is a pretty piece of property," I commented, looking at the stately oaks and rolling hills. A bit of blue water glistened in the distance. "Whose ranch is this, anyway?"

"Belongs to Marcie Auckland," he said as we wove through a grove of live oaks. "She was a judge in Houston before she retired."

We turned a bend and came up to a stately house built of the same limestone as the front gate. "There must be money in the family," I said. "Or this is a family property; government work doesn't pay enough to cover this."

"I don't know much about her family," he said, "but I'm sure someone does."

A fit woman with a cap of silvery hair rounded the house as Tobias parked the truck in the driveway. She wore muck-covered boots, a faded green T-shirt and jeans. Her lean, muscular arms belied a lot of time in a gym... or working outdoors.

"Here about the kid?" she asked as we got out of the truck. "I'm Marcie Auckland," she said, extending a callused hand.

"Lucy Resnick," I said.

"Come on back to the barn," she offered. "I've been bottle-feeding her, but I'm sure she'd like to get back to her mama."

Tobias and I followed her around the house and down a short path to the barn, a large wooden structure a ways from the house with a galvanized metal roof. It was painted a soft green, and was clearly a step above the utilitarian barn construction I was used to seeing in Buttercup. Again, there was money here.

"She's right in here," Marcie said as we followed her into the shady interior. She walked to a small stall on the right and opened the door.

My heart sank. The kid was around the right age, but it wasn't Cinnamon.

"It's not her," Tobias confirmed as he squatted down beside the kid. "When did she turn up?"

"Right after the storm," she said. "I don't have any other goats, so she's been kind of lonely."

Tobias did a quick check of the kid, palpating her abdomen and checking her over. "She's a little thin, but nothing broken or hurt. She's definitely a Nubian. I wonder where she came from?"

"Peter's got some Nubians," I said, "but the storm didn't hit his place. Maybe somebody strayed?"

"It's not that far from here," Tobias said. "I'll give him a call." He finished his exam and stood up. "I guess the big question is, what do you want to do with her?"

She eyed me. "I'm not really in the market for goats," she said. "If you want to take care of her, you can have her."

I looked at Tobias. "Do you think Carrot might accept her?"

"It's doubtful," he said, "but you could try. It would take a lot of time bottle-feeding, most likely."

"She looks awfully sweet," I said.

"They all do," Tobias said. "Until you're not watching, and then they're wreaking havoc. But you know that," he said, grinning at me.

"I do," I said. Most of the animals at Dewberry Farm seemed to have a streak of wanderlust, and I'd had to rescue Blossom, my Jersey cow, along with my goats Hot Lips and Gidget, from the Town Green more than once. I was getting tired of replacing the geraniums in the tubs flanking the Town Hall. "But they've been very good for a long time."

"This is the first town event they haven't visited, isn't it?"

"You mean the Easter Market?" I asked. "I think you're right."

"There's still time," the judge said with a wry smile. "Want to come in for some tea?"

"Sure," I said, "if Tobias has a few minutes."

"I do," he said.

"Good," Marcie said with a smile, "because I've got some cookies I need help eating."

The inside of the stone house was as lovely as the exterior, with golden pine flooring and white curtains on the huge windows. It was what I called "curated country," with several pieces that had been selected by an interior designer, I was guessing, along with what looked like a few family heirlooms, including a pie safe that looked a lot like the one I had inherited from my grandmother.

"I've got one just like this," I said.

"I love that piece," she told me as she poured us glasses of tea and set out some shortbread cookies on a plate. "I picked it up at the antique fair last year."

"How long have you been in the area?" I asked.

"Only a few years," she said.

"And you're a judge, I hear," I said as I sat down on one of the big leather couches in the living room.

"I was," she confirmed. "I'm retired. I hear you're going to have a judge as a neighbor soon, though," she said.

"What?"

"I heard a rumor the county judge—Todd McLain—was looking to move out of La Grange. I don't know if there's anything to it, but he might be your neighbor."

"Really?" I asked. "What do you know about him?"

Her mouth quirked down. "I don't know him well," she said stiffly.

Uh-oh. Something told me that she might not know him well, but what she did know she didn't much like. "Can you tell me anything?"

"He's an elected official," she said shortly. "Not for me to make judgments." She paused, taking a sip of her tea, and then added, "But he does seem to be acquiring rather a lot of property lately."

"Oh?" I asked.

"Someone might want to look into that," she said as she put a tray with cookies and tea on the coffee table.

I reached for a glass and took a sip; it was delightfully cool, with a touch of mint. "Why?"

She shrugged. "Judgeships, particularly in rural districts, usually aren't top-dollar positions." I glanced around at the lovely living room. "I know," she said, reaching for a shortbread cookie. "I live in a lovely place, and I'm lucky. But I worked as an attorney in private practice for twenty-five years. I did the government work as a way of giving back to the community."

That made more sense. "Well, you picked a lovely place to live," I said.

She smiled. "Thanks. It's a change from the city, but I'm enjoying it here. I've only been here about three years, but I think this will probably be my forever home."

"Mine too," I said, thinking that for a retiree, Marcie seemed rather up on things legal in Buttercup. "This is a total non sequitur, I know, but I understand someone was looking into Sunset Home. I know it's a long shot, but do you happen to know anything about that?"

"I did hear something about it, actually," she said. "Didn't the person who was looking into it die unexpectedly?"

"She did. How did you hear about it?"

"I met Eva down at the Blue Onion. Someone told her what I used to do, and she told me she thought the place wasn't being run very well, then asked me what I knew about filing lawsuits."

"What did you tell her?"

"I gave her the names of a few attorneys, but I never heard back from her."

"Would you mind telling me the names you gave her? I want to know if she moved ahead. This whole thing with Eva is bothering me, and I keep wondering if it might not be tied up with Sunset Home somehow."

"The thought had crossed my mind as well," Marcie said, giving me an approving look. "You're sharp."

"She used to be an investigative reporter for the *Chronicle*," Tobias told her.

"Ah. I'll bet you were good at it, too."

"She was," Tobias said. "And she's done a bit of investigating since coming to Buttercup, too."

"The bane of Rooster Kocurek's existence, from what I hear," Marcie said with a small grin.

"You know about that?"

"Who doesn't?" she said. "He's a blithering idiot. Thank heavens we've got Deputy Shames on the scene these days. And concerned citizens such as yourself."

"Thanks," I said. "You're making me blush. And I'm sorry we haven't met before."

"We have now," she said with a smile. "What brought you to Buttercup, anyway?"

"I think I've always been in love with it," I told her. "I came here as a kid... Dewberry Farm used to belong to my grandparents."

"You're lucky," she said. "My grandparents lived in

Detroit. I would have loved to have a place like this to come to. But I guess we can't be the architects of our childhoods, can we? All we can do is build our own futures."

"That's very true," I said. "And you've built something beautiful here."

"Thanks," she said. "Feel free to drop by anytime. It hasn't been as easy as I'd hoped meeting folks in town; a lot of them get nervous when they find out what my day job used to be."

I laughed. "Kind of like being a cop. Or an investigative reporter."

"Exactly," she said. "I'll be curious to see what you find out. Keep me posted, will you?"

"I will," I said. "And thanks so much for the help."

"I just hope it all gets figured out," she said. "And that you find your missing baby goat."

"Are you sure you're okay with us taking yours?"

"If that baby can find a mother, I think it would be best for everyone."

"You really think Carrot will take her?" I asked Tobias.

"Hard to say," he said. "I've got some tricks up my sleeve... but we'll have to cross our fingers."

∼

ALTHOUGH TOBIAS HAD a busy afternoon scheduled, he postponed a few appointments and drove both the kid and me back to Dewberry Farm; he'd had the presence of mind to toss a crate in the back of his truck.

"What do we do?" I asked when he pulled up outside the barn.

"We've got to make her smell familiar," he said. "Let's rub

Carrot and Thistle with a towel, and then rub down this little one so that she smells familiar."

"Okay," I said. "What else?"

"We probably want to cover her in some of Carrot's milk. And maybe rub her all over her future mom."

I wrinkled my nose. "Really?"

He nodded. "Really."

"All right," I said. "Whoever said farming was boring didn't know what they were talking about. I'll get a towel and milk her. What do we do with the other kid?"

"Let's start with her in there and see how it goes. I think we should tether Carrot, though, so she can't get too aggressive with the new one."

"Aggressive?"

"It can happen. I know she's pretty good-natured, but it's easier to do this when the kids are just born. Still, there's a chance it will take."

"You think?"

"It may be kind of hard for a while, and we may have to take Thistle out of there, but we'll give it a shot."

We spent the next thirty minutes "preparing" the new kid as much as we could. Then, once Tobias had rubbed the squirming kid all over Carrot and Thistle, it was time for the moment of truth.

"Ready?" he asked.

"Ready as we can be, I suppose." He set the little one down in the stall, nudging her toward Carrot, and then backed away, closing the door behind him.

If I was hoping for a quick, heartwarming moment of connection—which, in truth, I was—I was quickly disappointed. Carrot took one look at the newcomer and attempted to butt her away. Thistle soon followed suit, shoving the new arrival to the corner of the stall.

"This doesn't bode well," I said.

"Give it some time," Tobias suggested.

Unfortunately, ten minutes later, it was still the same situation. The new kid would approach Mom, only to be rebuffed with a bleat and as much of a shove as she could manage. As the new kid stood in the corner, looking forlorn, I started to open the door, intent on rescuing her.

Tobias put a hand on my arm. "No," he cautioned me. "We have to let them work it out."

"What if it doesn't work out?"

"Then we'll keep bottle-feeding her," he said. "But give it time."

As we watched, the new arrival made another go at sidling up to Carrot. Thistle was nursing on the other side, and the new kid managed to latch on for a moment or two before Carrot realized what was happening and shoved her away again.

"Is that progress?" I asked.

"It could be," he said. "We should probably give her a name, don't you think?"

"Let's see who she is first," I said.

"I hate to leave you, but I've got to head back to the clinic," Tobias said, giving me a kiss on the forehead. "Keep an eye on her. I'd do a supplementary feeding in a few hours just to be sure, but we need to see if they manage to bond."

"Should I stay here and watch?"

"You don't have to be right here all the time," he said, "but I'd check in from time to time."

"Got it," I said, watching the lonely little goat in the corner of the pen. "I hope it works. But what if we find Cinnamon? Can she handle three kids?"

"Let's deal with that as it comes," he said. "I'll check in later, okay?"

"Thanks," I said.

He gave me a quick kiss and headed back to his truck.

~

SADLY, it did not appear to be a case of love at first sight in the goat pen. After watching for about a half hour, I headed inside to process the day's milk and get some goat cheese going. I was milking, and although I was saving a lot of it for the kids, there was enough to make quite a bit of cheese; I was glad to be able to put several new rounds into the fridge that afternoon.

When I finished cleaning up, I looked up the names of the attorneys Marcie had given me. Unfortunately, that was a dead end; no one would even tell me if Eva had been a client. I had just hung up, trying to figure out how else to get info out of them, when the phone rang. It was Jennifer.

"Are you doing okay?" I asked her.

"No. Yes. I don't know." Her voice was rough, as if she'd been crying.

"I'm so sorry," I told her. "It's been a pretty awful week for your family."

"It has," she agreed. "And I just left Faith Zapalac's office."

"What's the news on the house?"

"She said there's no way for the seller to get out of the contract. She didn't want to talk to me at all, in fact... kept trying to push me out the door."

"Have you talked with your mom?"

"She isn't sure she can afford to keep the house. I have to go over to see if I can find the account statements this afternoon; she has no idea what her financial situation is. And I may have to hire an attorney."

"I think whoever has the contract on your mom's house has bought a lot of properties recently," I said.

"What are you thinking?"

"I don't know yet," I said, "but it may be linked to a local judge, and local judges aren't usually raking in the big bucks." Nor was I overly confident in Faith Zapalac's moral compass.

It was time to talk to Dottie again.

16

When I got to Sunset Home, there was no one at the front desk. I glanced around, then hurried behind the desk and opened the first binder I saw. It was a list of amenities and schedules, but the second one had a list of patients, their rooms, and their legal guardians. Jerri Roswell was listed as guardian for at least a dozen names. I snapped a quick pic of each page with my phone, and was just hurrying back around to the front of the desk when the receptionist reappeared from the hallway. She gave me a suspicious look.

"I'm here to see Dottie Kreische," I announced breezily as I turned left to head down the hallway.

"Wait..." she said. "Who are you?"

"I know where it is," I told her. As I walked briskly away from the reception desk, a man with a stethoscope emerged from Dottie's room. He was chatting with a woman I recognized: Jerri.

"Is Dottie okay?" I asked, hurrying down the hallway.

"Who are you?" the man asked.

"She's not a relative," Jerri said. "In fact, I'm not sure why she's here. I'm not sure she's authorized."

"Authorized?" I asked. "Since when do you have to be authorized to visit a friend?" I pushed past them and into Dottie's room.

My friend was lying on the bed, looking—for lack of a better word—cadaverous. Her face was drawn and waxy, and her chest barely moved, her breathing almost imperceptible.

"What's wrong with her?" I asked, looking up at the doctor and Jerri. "What did you give her?"

"She was experiencing agitation," Jerri said smoothly. "I called Dr. Frederick. He gave her a sedative to help her sleep."

"She was fine yesterday," I protested.

"She's suffered a major loss," Jerri pointed out. "Grief can be agitating... sometimes our patients become a danger to themselves."

I looked down at Dottie. How could I keep her safe?

"I really think it's time you left," Jerri said shortly.

"You're not her guardian," I said. "And you're not the administrator here, either. I turned to the portly man with her. "You must be Dr. Frederick. How did you come to be Dottie's doctor? She's never mentioned you."

"Dr. Frederick is our attending physician," she said.

"*Our?* I thought you were just a guardian. Are you affiliated with the nursing home, too? That sounds like it could be a conflict of interest."

She gave me a sour look.

"Be that as it may, I am the attending physician, and I think it's time for you to leave," the doctor said in a gravelly voice that held a note of warning. He fixed me with a level gaze. "Ms. Kreische needs her rest."

"I'm calling her daughter first," I said, reaching into my bag for my cell phone. Jerri and the doctor exchanged glances. As I scrolled through the numbers, I added, "I hear you and Eva Clarke had a bit of a falling out."

"Eva Clarke's relationship with Sunset Home is the purview of human resources," Jerri said shortly. "Now, I think it's time you left before I have to call the authorities."

I crossed my arms. "Like I said, you have no legal right here."

"I think the administrator would disagree with you."

"Call the administrator, then. I have a few questions I'd like to ask. In the meantime, I'll just wait for Dottie's daughter to arrive." I parked myself in the visitor's chair and dialed as Jerri and the doctor stood in the doorway watching me.

Jennifer answered the phone on the third ring. "Hi, Jennifer? It's Lucy."

"Everything all right?"

"I'm in your mom's room at Sunset Home right now, with the doctor." I glanced up at Jerri and Dr. Frederick, who were exchanging meaningful glances. "They sedated your mother."

"Sedated?"

"She's completely out of it," I said.

"I'm getting her out of there," Jennifer said. "Can I do that?"

Jessie had had power of attorney, or maybe more, but he was dead, so it seemed to me that Dottie would no longer be subject to anyone else's whim. "I can't think why you wouldn't, if she wants to go." As long as the sedation wore off, that was.

Jerri murmured something to the doctor; I couldn't catch it, but I thought I heard the word "ward."

"I'll be there as fast as I can," she said.

"I'll wait," I told her, staring hard at Jerri.

"Thanks, Lucy," Jennifer gushed. "You've been wonderful."

We hung up a moment later, and I sat back in my chair, crossing my arms.

"You really aren't authorized to be here," Jerri repeated. "And the doctor has asked you to leave."

"I don't think I need authorization," I said. "Unless you've already managed to make yourself Dottie's new guardian. That's what you do, isn't it?"

Jerri's face went pale. "I don't know what you're talking about," she said.

"You're the doctor for all of Jerri's wards, aren't you?" I asked the man with the stethoscope. "That's the arrangement here, isn't it? Someone researches people without much family, Jerri takes over their finances, you get them moved here so you get a kickback from Sunset Home, you label them as incapacitated, and then Faith sells their property."

"That's ridiculous," she said, but her eyes were darting around the room.

"You've got the judge in your back pocket, too, don't you?"

"Don't say anything," the doctor warned her.

"That's why you drugged up Dottie," I said. "She knows too much. She was asking questions of the wrong people. You have to keep her quiet. How many of your other wards are kept tranquilized twenty-four seven? It keeps them quiet and pliant. And you've somehow managed to cut out any family members. That's the piece I haven't figured out yet."

"You're crazy," Jerri said.

"Faith's part of it, too, isn't she?" I asked.

"You need to leave," Jerri said. "Right now."

"Want me to call the police for you?" I asked, picking up my phone. "Because I will."

Her mouth formed a thin line. She looked like she was about to respond, then changed her mind. "Let's go," she said, and just about yanked the doctor out of the room after her.

I waited until they were gone, then poked my head out into the hall. There was no sign of them. I knew Dottie's friend Anna Neukirch was in the next room—Dottie had told me about her. With Dottie's door open, I quietly knocked. When Anna answered, I slipped into the room.

"Lucy!" Anna said, her brown eyes bright in her weathered face. "I'm so glad to see you. There was a hullabaloo with Dottie a few hours ago. Is she okay?"

"They drugged her up," I said. "Dottie told me you were in trouble; that you'd lost your rights."

Her eyes flashed. "Jerri got that doctor to declare me incompetent and then took over all of my property. She put me here and sold my house for almost nothing."

"That's horrible!" I said.

She nodded grimly, her eyes looking haunted. "I can't see my daughter, and I know Jerri's making a fortune off me. I was the one working with Eva. They've been keeping me on some kind of drug ever since; I just stopped taking them and spit them all out now. Eva was going to do something about it, but then..."

"Let's call Mandy Vargas down at the *Buttercup Zephyr*." As I reached for my phone, I heard the sound of footsteps in the hall. Anna and I locked eyes.

"Go check on her," Anna whispered.

I nodded and hurried out the door. Sure enough, it was

Jerri, with a security guard at her side, marching down the hall.

"Ma'am? I'm going to have to ask you to leave," the guard said to me.

"Why?"

"This is private property. You're trespassing."

"I'm here to visit my friend. I believe I have a right to do that."

"Ms. Roswell said you were causing a disturbance and were a threat to the residents," she said. "I'm afraid I'm going to have to ask you to leave."

"I'm afraid Dottie Kreische may be in danger," I told the guard. "I'd like to talk to the administrator."

"I'm sure she'll be fine," the guard said. "Now, let's go."

"No," I said. I walked into Dottie's room and sat down on the visitors' chair. "Call the police if you want me to leave. Heck, I'll call them myself," I said.

The security guard looked at Jerri.

"I'll handle this," Jerri said, and with a shrug, the guard left the room. Jerri waited, dry lips pursed, until the woman had walked down the hall and rounded the corner before turning to me. "What do you want?" she asked.

"What do you mean, what do I want?"

"How much?" she asked.

"How much?" I repeated. "You want to buy me off?"

"Look," she said, giving her head a slight, contemptuous shake; her dark bobbed hair didn't move. "These people are at the ends of their lives. They have no family; they're just winding down their last bits of time. What we do is a service to them. If they didn't have us, who would they have?"

"I talked with a resident who told me family isn't even allowed to visit."

As I spoke, she looked down at her phone and sent a quick text.

"Who are you texting?" I asked.

"Just my daughter," she said breezily. "Seriously, though," she said, leaning forward in a conspiratorial way. She smelled strongly of perfume and antiseptic. "I hear you're a farmer. That's got to be a hard business. Wouldn't, say, five hundred or a thousand a month go a long way to help?"

She was looking to bribe me. "What would you say the payments were for?" I asked.

She shrugged. "Maybe you could provide our residents with some organic produce," she said. "It would be good for their health, I'm sure. We care very much about the well-being of our clients."

"I can tell," I said drily, glancing at Dottie's waxen face.

"Seriously," she said. "Why not? They're not around for long. We give them a good life. They don't have families, so the money would just go to waste anyway."

"What about Dottie?" I asked. "She's got family."

"She and her daughter have been estranged for years," she said. "She won't care."

"You can tell her that when she gets here," I said.

17

Dottie was starting to come to when Jennifer arrived. Jerri had backed off, and once Jennifer had started the process of getting her mother out of the home and under proper care, I headed back to the farm, where I pulled out my laptop as Chuck curled up on my feet. I Googled Dr. Frederick; he'd moved to Buttercup five years ago, after leaving a geriatric practice in Houston. Then I started going through the names on the list of residents I'd photographed at Sunset Home and ran them through the Fayette County Appraisal District. Of the first ten names I ran, four of them had owned property in Fayette County, but sold it in the last five years. I wrote down the names of the properties, wondering if Mandy could figure out who had handled the transactions—or how much the homes had sold for. And to whom.

My next job was to Google Jerri Roswell. Her name came up as the owner of Safe Hands Guardians, which (according to its very basic website) was a guardianship company based out of La Grange. There were no references, just a list of services, including financial stewardship and managing medical care, and no staff listed other than Jerri. When I Googled the company to find out when it was established, I wasn't surprised to discover that it had come into being at about the same time Jerri moved to Buttercup.

I flipped back to the search results and ran through the first few pages, then discovered a small news article published ten years before. Evidently Jerri had been doing guardianship longer than five years; according to the short article, which had appeared in a Bastrop newspaper, a family named Martin had sued her for guardianship of an elderly member of the family. "We had no idea what happened," the woman in the article, the elderly woman's granddaughter, said. "One day we went to visit Grandma and there was a for sale sign in the yard. Someone we had never met was inside sorting through her things, and my grandmother had been moved to a low-rent nursing home in San Antonio. We weren't even allowed to see her."

By the time I got off the computer, I was even more certain about what was happening at Sunset Home.

I picked up the phone and called Mandy at the *Buttercup Zephyr*.

"I was just about to call you," she said. "The outfit that is buying the property next door to you is called Buttercup Holding. I can't find out who all owns it, though; I think it's a shell company. I did find one local name connected with it, though."

"Whose?"

"Faith Zapalac set it up.

Again, I thought of what was written on the piece of paper in Eva's pocket: *Cup Holding*. It made sense.

"I think I've got a scoop for you," I said. "But I need you to find out a few more things, if you can."

"Tell me," she said.

"Can you find out who the presiding judge was for the guardianships at Sunset Home?"

"I can tell you already," she said. "Guardianships are all handled by the county judge; his name is Todd McLain. He got himself into a bit of a scandal over campaign contributions a few years ago; we ran a story on it. Nothing came of it, but where there's smoke..."

"I heard a rumor that a judge is buying the property through Buttercup Holdings," I said. "If that's who it is, I'll bet he's tied up in all of this, too. I think they're working together to declare vulnerable older folks without much family incompetent, putting them in Sunset Home, having Jerri take control of their assets and selling their real property to Buttercup Holding at a discount price."

"That's horrible!" Mandy said, but I could hear the excitement of a reporter on a scoop. "I've read a few articles about that happening in other places... but here in Buttercup?"

"I know," I said. "I wish it weren't true. And we haven't proven it yet. It's just a theory."

"A strong theory," she pointed out. "I'll see if I can connect Judge McLain to Buttercup Holding. Do you think any of this has something to do with the murders?"

"I don't know. Everything leads back to Sunset Home," I said, "and Dottie just moved there. But Jerri Roswell, the county judge, Dr. Frederick... I think they're all involved somehow. I have a list of the folks who are at Sunset Home, including the ones who are under Jerri Roswell's guardianship. She owns Safe Hands Guardians, and I'm guessing she sold all their properties. Can you do a search and find out who bought them?"

"I can," she said. "But what does that have to do with

killing Eva? Dottie had nothing to do with Buttercup Holding."

"No, but Jessie was working with Faith, and Buttercup Holding put in the offer for her property. Plus, I think Eva was looking to whistle-blow; that would be a good motive for any of them."

"What about Jessie, then?"

"I don't know," I confessed. "Did he find out what was going on, somehow? I know he lost his job recently; did he figure out what was going on and want in on the action, maybe?"

"I'll see if I can dig up a connection," she said.

"I'll get in touch with my contacts in Houston, too. We'll see what we can find out, and then we'll decide what to do with it."

"I'm planning on running the story," Mandy told me.

"I know," I said. "The question is, is Rooster more likely to listen to us before or after it runs?"

"Let's get the facts together first," she said.

"I'm worried," I told her. "Jerri Roswell tried to bribe me to keep me quiet. If she killed Eva and Jessie, what if I'm next in line?"

"You don't own a gun, do you?"

"No," I said.

"You might want to reconsider."

∾

I LEFT a message for one of my former colleagues in Houston and headed outside to clear my head. The whole mess was on my mind as I went out to plant the rest of my vegetable starts; the sooner I got them in, the better. I stopped to check on the new kid along the way; as before, she was huddled in the far corner of the stall, looking lonely, while Carrot and Cinnamon were holed up in the opposite corner. Tobias had been optimistic, but I wasn't so sure. I left the stall with a sigh. I'd been checking in on the new arrival, who I'd named Niblet, but it didn't look like there was any progress on the bonding front.

The sun was high in the sky and there was a cool breeze, making it a perfect spring day as I busied myself putting in broccoli starts in, but my thoughts were dark. As I tucked the new plants into the freshly turned soil, I found myself wondering what Mandy was going to discover... and about Jerri Roswell. Had she killed Eva to keep her guardianship business going? That I could see... but what about Jessie? Had he found out about what Jerri was up to? Had she offered to pay him off, and had he refused? Or had his blackmail offer been too high for her to accept?

Or had he killed Eva to prevent her from taking over his mother's estate, and then been killed by Edward out of revenge? I didn't like to think about that, but the anger in Edward's voice when I'd spoken with him had been hard to ignore.

I had finished one row and was starting the next when my phone rang. It was Molly.

I wiped my hand on my jeans and answered. "What's up?"

"Ethan didn't come home from school," she said.

I glanced at my watch; it was late afternoon. School had ended at least an hour earlier.

"I assume he's not in any after-school activities?"

"No," she said. "He didn't come home on the bus, and Brittany said she didn't see him after school. And he's not answering his phone."

"I'm sure he's fine," I said soothingly, but my stomach

clenched. Had he gone to Edward's house with his friend June after class?

Was Edward a murderer?"

"Have you talked to Edward?" I asked, trying to keep my voice calm.

"I don't have his number," she said. "Do you?"

"Unfortunately, I don't."

"I'm about to go over there."

"I'll go with you," I offered, still feeling that creeping dread. "I'm heading to the truck right now."

18

Molly was standing outside the door of her house waiting for me when I pulled up ten minutes later.

"I'm sure Ethan is fine," I reassured her as she got into the truck. After all, I reasoned to myself, even if Edward was a murderer, he'd have no reason to do anything to Molly's son. Unless he'd found out something that would implicate his friend's dad...

I pushed the thought aside and hit the gas; a few minutes later, we were pulling into the driveway of Edward's place. I recognized his red van in the driveway, but there was no sign of June or Ethan.

We hurried out of the truck and knocked on the door. Molly looked pale, and I reached out to squeeze her arm.

Edward was wearing a paint-covered apron when he opened the door. He looked confused to see the two of us on his doorstep. "Everything okay?"

"Is your daughter here?" Molly asked.

"I don't think so," he said, glancing back over his shoulder. "June!" He called. "June Bug!"

No answer.

"Did she come home from school?"

"I was painting," he said. "I kind of lost track of time... Junie!"

Again, nothing.

"Come on in," he said. "Did something happen?"

"My son didn't come home from school today," Molly said in a clipped tone. "I was wondering if he and your daughter were off somewhere together."

Edward sighed. "Kids. They have their own agendas, don't they?"

"I'd like to know what their agenda is, frankly," Molly said as she perched on a beaten-up couch in Edward's cluttered living room. I sat down next to her. Edward moved a couple of books on art from a derelict rocking chair across from us and slid into it; the whole house smelled strongly of paint and solvent. "They've been spending a lot of time together, I hear. Including at night."

Edward's eyebrows rose. "You think they're more than friends?"

"I don't know what they are," Molly said, "but sneaking out at night and drinking in the barn isn't acceptable behavior in my house."

Edward bristled, and there was a dangerous glint in his eye. "Who says it's acceptable in mine?"

"I'm sorry," Molly said, raking a hand through her graying hair. "I'm just... upset. I don't know where Ethan is, and I don't know what he's been up to lately, and he and your daughter spend a lot of time together."

"It sure sounds like you're blaming June Bug for whatever it is your son is getting into. Could be the other way around, you know."

Molly's hands tightened on her phone; I could see the

knuckles whiten. She took a deep breath and said, "You're right. But right now, we don't know where either of them is. And I have a bad feeling about it."

Edward said nothing, but a shadow of worry passed over his face.

"Do you know where they go when they hang out?" Molly asked.

"There's an old barn out in the back," he said. "I keep tools and big stuff out there; I mainly use it for storage. I know June likes to spend time out there, but I don't know if she and Ethan hang out there together."

"Let's go look," I suggested, and Molly and I followed Edward out to the back of the little house.

The barn was a weathered building with a rusted, corrugated-metal roof, and a decided slant to it.

"Is this safe?" Molly asked as Edward pulled up on the latch and opened the silvery wood double door at the end of the building. The long grass had been beaten down around the entrance; it was obvious that someone visited the barn often.

"Hasn't fallen down yet," he said. He seemed totally unconcerned compared to Molly. Was it just grief over Eva? Or was he just a much more laissez-faire parent?

We stepped into the barn behind him; beyond the square of light illuminated at the entrance, the inside was striped with light from the gaps between the boards. It took a moment for my eyes to adjust, but once they did, I could make out a jumble of old lumber, rusted lawnmowers, and junk. Molly's lips were a tight, thin line, and I found myself wondering if I was up-to-date on my tetanus shots.

"Ethan?" she called, stepping over a rusted metal pail. "Ethan? June? Anyone there?"

Nobody answered, and together we followed what

looked like a path through the debris. It led to a far corner of the barn, where something of a sitting area had been constructed from an old futon and a couple of crates. I walked over and peered under the futon, pulling out a Mason jar with a few dead cigarettes inside of it and an empty beer can. It was a Lone Star, which I knew was Molly's husband Alfie's favorite beer.

"Well, we found the hangout," I said, bending down again to see what else had been hidden under the futon.

"But where are the kids?"

None of us knew.

I walked around a minute more, and spied an old safe half-hidden behind an old dryer. A shiny padlock held it shut.

"Is this yours?" I asked Edward.

"No," he said, shaking his head.

"Do you have a bolt cutter?"

"In my workshop. I'll be back in a minute," he said, and headed back along the cluttered path toward the door.

When he was out of sight, Molly turned to me. "I can't believe how negligent he is! These kids are smoking, drinking..." She jabbed a finger at the beer can. "He had no idea what was going on back here, and never even thought to check. We're lucky it's just beer and cigarettes."

My eyes slid to the safe. It was just beer and cigarettes so far, I thought but didn't say. Something told me we'd find out more about what June and Ethan were up to once Edward cut that bolt.

"It doesn't look great," I admitted.

"Not great? Not great?" Molly crossed her arms. "He's forbidden to see that girl ever again."

"Let's get all the facts first," I said, putting a hand on her arm. "I met her; she seemed like a nice girl, and Ethan generally has a good head on his shoulders. We don't know what they've been up to; maybe Ethan has been spending his time here because Edward's a working artist."

"He's obviously not working here in the barn," she hissed.

"I know it's upsetting. But let's find out what we can and talk to them before you make any proclamations. Besides, if you're worried about them being here, you can always have June over to your house."

Before she could answer, Edward appeared at the door of the barn. "Found them," he said, and wove back through the debris to where we were standing.

It took two tries to cut the bolt. Edward slipped it off and opened the door.

Inside were several cans of white spray paint and a stack of papers.

"What are those?" Molly asked.

"Looks like flyers of some sort," Edward said. "Something about animal rights?"

"Those are the letters on the barns," I said, taking one from the stack.

Edward blinked at me. "What barns?"

"The ones that have been spray-painted," I said.

"Oh, God," Molly moaned. "They're vandals. That's what they've been doing."

"For a cause, I suspect," I said, handing her a flyer. As Edward and Molly read the flyers, which talked about cruelty to animals and the horrors of feedlots (which I couldn't disagree with), I bent down and peered into the safe. There was a spiral-bound notebook with the letters SAAC in block print on the front. I opened it and found the words SOCIETY AGAINST ANIMAL CRUELTY in block print on the first page.

"Well, at least we know what SAAC stands for," I said. On the next page was a list of local ranches, all of which I knew were of the "factory-farming" approach. Several had been crossed off; I recognized three of them as ranches I knew had been hit with spray paint and animals let out of their pens.

"So that's what they were doing late at night," Molly said.

"Seems so," I said.

"Is that where they are now, then, do you think?"

"I doubt it," I said. "It's still light, and the spray paint is in the safe."

"They could be doing reconnaissance," Edward suggested.

"True. I wish there were some way of figuring out where they could be," Molly said.

"Do you have a map of Buttercup?" I asked.

"Why?" Molly asked.

"Mandy Vargas just did an article on the vandalism around town. There were dates in it; I figured if we had a map and could match up dates and locations, we might be able to figure out where they're going next."

"But we don't know if that's what they're doing," Molly objected.

"We don't," I said, "but they're out there somewhere, and it's the only idea I have."

"I can't argue with that," Edward said. "Come inside and I'll print a map of the area. It's better than any idea I can come up with."

We followed him into the house. Molly still looked worried, but I sensed a bit of relief, too. Social justice warrior seemed to be easier to swallow than vandal. Although I suspected there would still be a conversation about the beer can and the cigarette butts.

Assuming we found them. Which, of course, we would. Right? I glanced over at Edward. Had he killed Eva and Jessie? Were we working together with a murderer?

"There's sparkling water in the fridge," he offered as he opened up his laptop and pulled up a map of Buttercup.

"Thanks," I said. "You want one?"

"Sure," he said, and I grabbed three from his cluttered fridge as he printed up the map.

"I don't know where these ranches are," he said as he peered at the network of roads.

"We do," Molly said, reaching for it. He handed it over to her.

"Can you pull up the *Zephyr* article?" I asked.

"Sure," he said. His fingers flew across the keyboard; a moment later, the article appeared. He printed it, then handed it to me.

"Okay," I said, taking a sip of fizzy water and studying the article. "The first incident was at Ed Zapp's, with the chickens," I said, "and it was a month ago." I read off the date.

"Got it," Molly said, making an X and a date on the map.

"The second was a week later, at the Froehlichs' place." She marked down that one, as well as the rest of the incidents. When she was done, we took a look at the map.

"They're all pretty close to you," I said, marking Edward's house with an X. "Three on Giddings Road, one on Mueller, and one on Church Road."

"All within a couple of miles of here," Molly said. "It makes sense; neither of them can drive."

"Which means they're probably working alone," I surmised. "And the last incident was about a week ago, so if the pattern fits, they'll likely do another tonight."

"I already called down to the station to tell them I hadn't

seen Ethan," Molly said. "Should I tell them about this, too?" she asked.

"If it were anyone but Rooster, I'd say yes. I don't think he'll be much help, and I'd rather find them and talk to them first. Maybe they can make restitution to the ranch owners without getting the police involved."

"That would be good," Molly said. "But what if they're not there? What if someone shoots them? And why isn't Ethan answering his phone?"

"We'll head out now to see if we can find them. In the meantime, keep trying to reach him," I said. "Let's plot the other ranches on this map. We'll go to the ones we think are the issue; if we haven't had any luck, we'll call the police and tell them everything we've put together. Sound like a plan?"

They both agreed, and together we plotted the remaining ranches on the map. There were only four more within what appeared to be walking distance.

"Let's split up," I said.

"I'll go to the Gunthers' ranch," Molly said. "They're friends of ours."

"I know where this one is," Edward volunteered, pointing to a sprawling ranch a little farther out.

"And I'll take Fred Smolak's place," I said. "I've got Molly's number, but Edward, we both need yours."

Once we'd exchanged numbers, we headed out, Molly texting her son one more time.

As I climbed into my truck, I felt a frisson of fear. It took three tries to start it; I'd have to get the starter checked out, but now was not the time. I was pretty sure I was right about where Ethan and June had gone. But I was worried that something very bad had happened.

I put the truck in reverse and hoped I was wrong.

19

Fred Smolak's ranch was only a few miles from Edward's house. Although there was a barbed wire fence, the gate was open—it wouldn't be hard to walk in—with no cameras that I could see. There was a new "For Sale" sign tacked to the fence—the agent, of course, Faith Zapalac. I was surprised; I knew Fred had been in the area for a long time, and it surprised me that after all these years he'd consider moving. Was he giving up the ranch and moving into town? I wondered as I rolled down the driveway, keeping my eyes peeled for any sign of June or Ethan. The outbuildings, which included a few small corrugated metal barns, didn't appear to be tagged by spray paint.

I pulled up to the main house and got out of the car, then walked up to the front door. It was a 50s ranch house built with mustard-colored brick. I knocked on the door, but no one answered. I peeked through the door, but nobody was there. I walked around the back of the house. Several black cows grazed in the pasture. I scanned the area, but there was no sign of Ethan and June.

I knocked on the back door, hoping someone would

answer, but evidently Fred wasn't home. There was no sign of any life outside of the cows, in fact. Just to be sure, I called out the kids' names. "June! Ethan!"

There was a thump from somewhere.

"Hello?" I called, trying to identify the sound.

Nothing.

"June! Ethan!" I repeated. "Are you there?"

Again, a thumping sound. It wasn't coming from the house; it was coming from one of the outbuildings.

"Is someone there?" I called.

Another thump, a little less loud. It was coming from what looked like an old smokehouse out in the corner; it was built with concrete blocks and sported a rusted, corrugated metal roof. I walked toward it cautiously. Was there an animal trapped inside? Or maybe the kids?

"Is someone in there?" I asked as I got within a few yards of the little building. Now I heard something else... like a muffled voice. Had the kids hidden in the smokehouse and gotten trapped? I wondered. The door was latched on the outside; maybe they'd shut it and were unable to get out.

Cautiously, I lifted the latch on the wooden door and pulled it open.

Two scared teenagers stared back at me from the floor, where someone had trussed them up with duct tape and gagged them with bandannas.

"Oh, lord," I said. "Are you okay?"

June nodded, whites showing around her eyes.

"Let me get you undone," I said. "I'm going to wedge the door open first, though." A few feet from the door was a chunk of limestone. I pulled it over and used it to prop the door open, then hurried over to pull off their gags. Both of them gasped for breath as I busied myself with the duct tape. It wasn't budging.

"I have to go get my pocket knife out of the truck," I said. "I'll be right back."

I hurried to get my Swiss Army knife out of the glove compartment and came back, slicing at the silvery tape. June was first, and she rubbed at her wrists as I pulled off the tape, then recounted what had happened.

"We came over just to look at the place. We didn't do anything wrong. I promise."

"I wasn't saying you did," I reassured her. "What happened while you were here?"

"Well, we were checking out the barn, and two big SUVs came up the driveway, a white one and a black one.

"The black one was a Land Cruiser," Ethan supplied.

I thought of the black SUV I'd seen in the photo of Dottie's house at Edward's. I knew Faith Zapalac had a white Escalade; had they been there together, scoping the place out, when Edward snapped the picture? "What happened next?" I asked.

"Well, we hid behind the barn, of course. These ladies got out of their SUVs. One of them was blonde, and she was talking to the other one about selling the house. And how they paid some guy something to get some paperwork, and that all they needed was a doctor to sign off on something and it was a done deal. There was something about a court date and a judge, but I didn't catch that."

The doctor was Dr. Frederick, no doubt. I was sure he was the person they were using to declare the residents incompetent so they could assign them to a guardian who would sweep in and take over all their financial interests. Jerri Roswell.

"How did you end up in here?" I asked.

June turned to Ethan. "They started toward the barn. Ethan tripped over a rock when we were trying to get out of sight. And then the blonde lady pulled a gun and asked us what we'd heard."

"We told her we didn't hear anything," Ethan broke in. "But she put us in here anyway."

"Has she been back?"

June shook her head. "Not yet."

"How long ago did this happen?"

"Right after school," June said.

"Well," I said, "let's get you out of here before she comes back. Sound like a plan?"

"Yes, please, ma'am, June said, and Ethan nodded vehemently. I finished cutting off the duct tape, and together we headed out toward the truck.

As June and Ethan crowded in beside me, I turned the key in the starter. Nothing happened.

"Shoot," I said, mindful of the teenagers in the truck.

"What's wrong?" June asked, her young voice edged with fear.

"It's not starting," I said. I tried again, but nothing happened. Then I reached for the phone and called Tobias's cell phone. Unfortunately, it went straight to voice mail.

As it beeped and I began to leave a message, June yelped. I turned back to see Faith Zapalac's Escalade bumping up the driveway.

"Tobias, it's Lucy. I'm at Fred Smolak's ranch. Faith Zapalac kidnapped Ethan and June and locked them in a shed here. My truck won't start and she's coming up the driveway. Call the police!"

As I hung up and dialed 911, the Escalade drew closer. After two rings, someone finally answered.

"What is your emergency?"

"I am at Fred Smolak's ranch on Church Road in Buttercup. I rescued two kids from a shed, but their kidnapper is coming back up the driveway now and my truck won't start."

"What is that address again?" the woman asked. As she spoke, the Escalade pulled up behind us and Faith flew out of the driver's seat, a gun in her hand pointed at me.

"Put it down," she barked.

"The address, ma'am?" asked the dispatcher.

"Church Road in Buttercup," I said.

"The number?"

I didn't remember, and it didn't matter.

"Put the phone down now!" Faith barked, her heavily lined eyes wild. As I set the phone on the dashboard, I could still hear the dispatcher. "Ma'am? Ma'am? Are you there, ma'am?"

Unfortunately, so could Faith.

20

"Get out of the car," Faith hissed.

I slowly opened the front door and stepped out. I glanced back at June and Ethan; they were cowering together on the other side of the seat.

"All of you," Faith clarified. They slid out after me, both milk-white.

"What are you going to do to us?" June asked in a quavering voice.

"I haven't decided that yet," she said. "Who were you calling?"

"Tobias," I said. "He didn't answer. I left him a message."

As soon as I spoke, the sound of the dispatcher's voice floated out of the cab of the truck. "Ma'am? Are you there, ma'am?"

"That doesn't sound like a message," Faith said, grabbing my phone. She stabbed at it, hanging up the call, then looking at the screen. "That's 911. So they know where we are. Which means you're coming with me. Let's go," she said, still holding my phone as she waved the gun toward her enormous white SUV. "One kid in the front, one kid in the back," she said. "You're driving, Lucy."

"Where?"

"Shut up and do what I say. Here are the keys," she said, tossing me an enormous key chain with a sparkly poodle attached to it. "Get in the driver's seat. Slowly. Try anything and I'll have to shoot one of these kids."

June yelped. "We didn't mean to do anything, really. We just heard Mr. Smolak was sending some of his cows to a feedlot, and we wanted to see if we could let them out or something."

"I don't care what you were doing," Faith said. "Just be quiet and don't do anything stupid. Now, get in." She herded June to the front passenger seat and Ethan to the back, then got into the back seat of the Escalade, right behind me. "Start the car," she ordered me. I turned the key in the ignition and the Escalade hummed to life, the dashboard lighting up like a Christmas tree.

At her direction, I turned the SUV around and headed back down the driveway. She ordered me to take a left, and for a moment I hoped we were going back to town; surely someone would notice me driving Faith's car with June in the front seat and wonder what was going on. But she didn't turn me toward town. Within ten minutes, we were pulling up into the driveway of Dottie's house. My heart leaped a little bit; if Tobias came to the house, he'd see Faith's Escalade in the driveway and know where we were. But we didn't stop in the driveway; she had me drive on past the house before stopping. Then she ordered Ethan to go out and open the doors of the big barn tucked in next to the backyard shed. "When you've got it open, go inside and stand at the back wall." My heart sank as he opened the door to expose the empty floor of the barn, and a moment later we—and the Escalade—were out of sight.

"Turn it off," Faith barked.

I briefly considered gunning the engine and crashing the Escalade into the back of the barn, but Ethan was standing right between the white circles of the headlight beams, and when I glanced over my shoulder, Faith had the gun trained on June.

My heart sank as I turned the key in the ignition, and the engine cut off.

"So what are we doing here?" I asked Faith as we sat in the semi-darkness of the barn.

"These kids turned up where they shouldn't have," Faith said.

"We didn't hear anything!" June protested.

"Lucy, what were you doing at Fred Smolak's ranch?" Faith asked me, ignoring the girl.

"I was looking for June and Ethan," I said. I turned to June. "I know what you and Ethan have been up to. I found your notebook, and the spray paint."

"What we did was for a good cause!" she protested, her eyes wide. "We didn't hurt anyone."

"Your parents are worried sick," I said, hoping that I would somehow prick Faith's conscience.

"Stop talking," the real estate agent ordered me, blinking hard. Her hand was tight on the gun. "I'm thinking."

I really didn't want her to think too much. I wanted to distract her, so I could figure out how to get out of there... and give Tobias time to maybe figure out how to track me down.

"Can we talk outside for a moment? I thought we might cut a deal."

She looked at me with interest, and I could tell I was on the right track. "A deal?"

"I need to expand my farm, but I'm short on cash."

The gun dropped a little bit. She turned to me, her eyes calculating. "How much are we talking? The house is already under contract."

"Just a chunk of land," I said. "If I can finance it, I'm willing to pay a premium. Maybe you could talk to the buyer to see if we can work something out?"

"How much are we talking?"

"Another ten acres," I said. "I'm happy to pay you a finder's fee, too."

She pursed her lips, considering.

"Can we go talk about this in the house?" I suggested.

She thought about it for a moment. "Can't hurt," she said. "But I have to do something with them so they don't run away."

"We can lock the barn from the outside, can't we? I'll go check."

"No," she said. "You stay here. I'll check." She gave me a hard look. "But if you try anything, I'm not afraid to use this gun."

"Understood," I said.

She opened the door of the Escalade and walked backward toward the barn doors. When she stepped out of the barn, I whispered, "I'm going to distract her as long as I can. See if you can get out somehow and run over to my house. The door's unlocked; go in and call the police and let them know what's going on."

They nodded, their faces pale.

"Come on out, Lucy," she said. "And no funny business, you two."

I let myself out of the SUV and walked to the doors of

the barn, trying to look confident and unconcerned. Which was a bit of a challenge with a deranged real estate agent leveling a gun at my head.

"Do you have a key to the house?" I asked. "I figured we could go have a cup of coffee in the kitchen, where we can keep an eye on the barn."

"There's a lock box on the front door," she said. "The code is 7572. If you try anything..." She looked meaningfully at the barn.

"Got it," I said, wondering how I was going to get us all out of this.

21

My heart pounded as I hurried around the house. The porch roof was still twisted up; although the storm had hit just a few days earlier, it felt like a lifetime ago. I punched the code with shaking fingers and fumbled with the key. I let myself into Dottie's house a moment later. Unfortunately, the only phone in the house was in the kitchen, so there was no way to contact the police without Faith seeing me. As I closed the front door behind me, I scanned the entry hall and the living room to the left, looking for something I could use as a weapon. Unfortunately, unless I could find some way to hide an umbrella in my pocket, I was out of luck.

I walked slowly to the kitchen and opened the back door. Faith bustled in and gave me her real estate smile, with a little bit of frosted lipstick on her front tooth. She'd locked two teenagers in the barn, and earlier had duct-taped them and gagged them, but you'd never know it from her chirpy, let's-make-a-deal demeanor.

"Let's sit at the kitchen table," she suggested.

I wanted to stretch things out as long as possible. "Mind if I make us some tea?" I suggested.

"I suppose," she said. She was still holding the gun, but it was no longer leveled at me. It was as if she'd forgotten it was there; the gun dangled almost casually from her right hand.

"I'll see if I can find some cookies, too," I said as I filled the teakettle with water and put it on the stove. "You've got a really good thing going, it seems," I added. "I'm glad Dottie is in a place where she's getting the care she needs."

"Yes. The home really is the best place for a lot of older folks. They just don't realize what's good for them."

"I know Eva was giving Dottie a hard time about moving, but it sounds like she was just really shortsighted," I said.

"I'm glad you can see that. She didn't understand that taking care of things for her and moving her to a better place was doing her a service." She shook her highlighted, carefully coifed head. "To be honest? I think she just didn't want to be out of a job. Jerri and I had everything all set up, but she just kept trying to stick her oar in. Same thing that happened with some of the residents at the home."

"Oh?" I said mildly as I found a box of butter cookies in one of the cabinets.

"She got fired for messing with things," Faith said. "She was interfering with what was best for the residents."

"I heard she got into a dustup with someone named Jerri," I replied. "She was in charge of a lot of the residents, wasn't she?"

"She is very efficient," Faith said. "If Jessie hadn't been around, I would have hooked Dottie up with Jerri. Fortunately, Jessie understood what was best for his mother."

"Did he call you, or did you approach him?"

She looked up at me and narrowed her blue eyes. "Why do you care?"

"You just have such a reputation," I said, backpedaling. "I'm sure you're the person everyone talks to when they're thinking of selling. You *are* Buttercup real estate."

She relaxed, and her lips curved into a smile. I took a deep breath and tried to calm my racing heart.

"Did you talk to Eva, try to get her to understand?"

"Oh, I did," she said. "It's a horrible thing to say, I know, but for Dottie's sake, it's a good thing Eva died when she did. Even though it's a real shame," she added woodenly. "I feel a little bad for her. It was a bad way to go."

"What do you mean?" I asked, feeling a chill. Nobody but Tobias, Deputy Shames and I knew how Eva had died. "Strangled by her own scarf," Faith said blithely, inspecting the gun and rubbing at a smudge on the barrel.

"Horrible," I murmured.

"Still," she said, in a weird, dreamy voice, "what's done is done."

"And then for Dottie's son to die so soon after," I said. "Who do you think killed him?" I asked, although I was pretty sure I already knew.

"I'll bet it was that man she was seeing. Edward something-or-other. I heard the other day that he thought Jessie had killed Eva." She nodded sagely, still watching the barn. "I mean, it's obvious. Jessie was killed right where Edward works. It was a revenge killing. It's the only thing that makes sense."

"You think?"

She nodded. "He probably led him there under false pretenses, then got rid of him."

"I'm sure once the police go through their phones, they'll be able to prove it," I said lightly.

"I heard they didn't have their phones with them," Faith said.

If I'd had any doubts at all, they were all gone now. "Even so," I said, "surely they'll be able to tell from phone records, won't they?"

"I doubt that will help," she said. "Everyone uses caller ID blocking these days."

If she'd blocked the number, why take the phones? Curiosity about who else her victims might have contacted? Or had she perhaps had earlier interactions with them—voice mails or texts—she wanted to keep under wraps?

"What kind of tea would you like?" I asked, hoping to keep her comfortable and distracted while I figured something out. I stole a glance at the barn. Had Ethan and June figured out how to get out? Had I made a mistake in recommending they try? Faith's eyes had barely left the barn since we got to the kitchen. "Here," I said, displaying the tea boxes, hoping to draw her attention away from the window. "Dottie's got peppermint, chamomile, and English breakfast."

"English breakfast," Faith said without looking. "With lemon, if you have any."

"I'll look," I said. I opened the fridge, relieved to find a wizened lemon on the top shelf. I took it out and put it on a small cutting board, then reached for a knife. I cut the lemon into wedges, then turned and made sure Faith's eyes were still trained on the barn before slipping it into the pocket of my jeans. I put a plate of cookies on the table along with a plate of lemon wedges and the sugar bowl, then sat down next to Faith as we waited for the water to heat.

"So," she said brightly. "Back to business. You want a piece of land?"

"I do," I said. "I know you already have the place under

contract, but do you think the buyer would be willing to do a deal?"

"It depends on how much you're willing to spend," she said.

"Who's the buyer?"

"It's an investment firm," she said.

My stomach lurched again. Which was saying something, considering I was sitting next to what I was pretty sure was an armed murderer and trying to keep her from killing my friend's child and his classmate.

"What kind of investment firm?" I asked. "What are they planning to do?"

"I don't think that's been nailed down yet," she said vaguely. "But I'm sure they'd be open to a strong offer. It's a hundred-acre parcel. I'm thinking we might be able to peel off ten acres on the west side of the lot," she said, biting her lip. "Not including the house, of course. It's premium property, though, so it won't be cheap, although I might be able to get you a bit of a discount."

"How much are we talking?" I asked.

She quoted me a price that was three times as much as I'd spent to buy the farm. I knew property prices had gone up, but that seemed ridiculous. Not that it mattered, frankly. My main concern was getting the kids out of the barn alive... and, if possible, me out of Dottie's house without being peppered with bullets.

"That seems like a lot," I said. "But I might be able to work it out." I took a breath. "Buttercup Holding has been buying a lot of properties, hasn't it? Did you help set it up?"

"I have a lot of clients," she said tightly, but she didn't deny it.

The kettle whistled, and I got up to pour into two cups. I put them on saucers with spoons, then carried them back to the table and set one in front of Faith. My hope was that she'd put down the gun long enough to squeeze lemon into her tea and stir it in.

She didn't.

"Squeeze one of those in there for me, will you?" she asked. "Sugar, too?" I did as she asked, and gave her tea a quick stir. "Thank you," she said. "Now," she went on, picking up the cup with her free hand and taking a small sip. Her voice had changed; she was out of real estate sales mode. "I have to decide what to do."

"What is there to do? Just let the kids go home. I'll vouch for you if they complain."

"But they heard things," she said, fingering the gun. "It's risky."

"Who's going to believe two kids?" I asked, feeling my heart race. "Just let them go. Whatever they heard can't have been that bad. Besides, you've been doing a service."

"I don't know," she said. All of a sudden, there was a shift in the feeling in the room. A shift I didn't like one bit.

"Have a cookie," I suggested. "Sugar always helps me."

She reached for a cookie mechanically. A phone in her pocket started vibrating; she fumbled in her pocket, pulled a phone out and looked at the screen. "There's a text that says they're on their way. Who's on their way? Where?" She stood up, gripping the gun.

"Whoever it is, I'm sure they're headed to Fred Smolak's ranch," I said. "You took the kids' phones when you found them, right?"

She nodded.

"None of us has had a phone since we were at Fred's place. We're safe here; the car's in the barn, and there's no one around."

"I don't know," she said. "Maybe I should take care of the

problem." Her eyes drifted to me, and there was a calculating look in them I didn't like at all. The barrel of the gun drifted toward me. "Who inherits your farm?"

As she spoke, there was a chill breeze and a whiff of lavender. A moment later, there was a crash from the front room.

Faith jerked and turned around, pointing the gun away from me, toward the sound of the crash. "What was that?"

"I don't know," I said, and slid my hand into my pocket. As Faith stood up, my fingers closed around the knife. She took a few steps toward the living room. I fell in behind her, mustering my courage as she scanned the room.

The mirror over the fireplace had come loose from its moorings, hitting the mantel and scattering photographs across the carpeted floor. "Not broken," Faith said as she lifted a corner of the mirror. "Good. No bad luck."

As she began to stand up, still off-balance in her pink high-heeled shoes, I felt my grandmother's presence.

Now.

I stepped forward and put the knife to Faith's back. "Drop the gun," I said in a voice that sounded like business, even though my hand was shaking.

"No," she said in a harsh voice. Her body whirled to the right, the gun swinging around toward me. The knife turned to the side. I reached for her wrist with my free hand, wrenching the gun away from me, but Faith was surprisingly strong. I held up the knife, not sure exactly where to put it as we wrestled. She might be trying to kill me, but I still felt squeamish about sticking a knife into another human being.

Unfortunately, she seemed to feel no such compunction.

"I should have killed you before," she snarled as I tried to figure out what to do with the knife.

"Like you did Jessie and Eva?" I asked as I pushed against her wrist, straining to keep the gun aimed away from my head.

"They had to die," she said. "They were ruining the whole setup."

"Even Jessie?"

"He found out from Eva. He was going to blackmail me, that dirty rat."

"I thought he and Eva were enemies?"

"She told him about the arrangement I had with Jerri and the doctor when she was trying to talk him out of selling the house. I was on the road to retirement in a few years... if he blew things up, all my plans would be destroyed."

"And then he figured you killed her and was blackmailing you to stay quiet?"

"Both. The set-up and Eva."

Even though I was struggling for my life, I reflected that Jessie never was the brightest bulb. Blackmailing a murderer? "I had to stop him," Faith continued. "And now you... this is not what I planned."

With a new burst of strength, she kicked my leg out from beneath me. The knife tumbled from my hand as I crumpled to the floor, still holding her wrist. I flailed for the knife with the other hand, but it was out of reach, and now Faith was bending over me, inching the gun closer to my head, her carefully made-up face distorted with rage, eyes bulging, lipsticked lips pulled back, exposing a line of yellowed teeth.

My eyes darted down to Faith's wobbly high-heeled shoes. She was off-balance. I heaved my body to one side and swept my leg into her ankles, still holding tight to her wrist. She let out a squeal and fell on top of me, her elbow digging into my stomach. I reached for her wrist with my other hand, but she still held tight to the gun, and was pushing it toward my head again.

As we wrestled, there was the sound of a car engine in the driveway. Faith looked up. "Did they get out of the barn?" Her arm relaxed for a split second—long enough for me to slam it against the corner of the coffee table.

"Ouch!" she yelled as the gun skittered across the rug.

I heaved her off me and threw myself at the gun, but as my hand closed on it, something stabbed into my shoulder.

Faith had the knife.

I jerked my hand back instinctively, and she lunged for the gun. Feeling a searing pain in my shoulder, I shot out my arm and managed to shove it under the coffee table just in time. She squealed in anger and frustration and pulled back my hair; a second later, I felt cold metal bite at my throat.

"No," I gasped just as the front door flew open.

22

"Drop it," came a voice I recognized, but couldn't place.

"What are you doing here?" Faith asked in a hysterical voice.

"Drop it," the voice repeated.

"No." Faith's voice was gravelly. The knife bit in harder. Where was my jugular? How long would it take me to bleed out if she cut it?

And who had walked into Dottie's house?

Despite the knife digging into my throat, I tilted my head so I could see the door.

It was Jennifer, and she was leveling a shotgun at Faith.

"What on God's green earth are you doing, Faith? I thought you were a good Christian woman!"

"This has nothing to do with that," Faith said. "Just walk away and let me tidy things up."

"Tidy things up?" Jennifer said. "Oh, wait. You tidied up my brother, too, didn't you? And poor Eva?"

Faith said nothing.

"You were going to make a tidy packet on Mother's

house, weren't you? And Eva didn't want you to, so you killed the poor woman who was trying to look after my mother."

"Shut up," Faith said. "Shut up, shut up, shut up."

"I can't believe this," Jennifer said. "What did my brother do? Threaten to give the listing to someone else? You're a piece of work."

"I'll kill her. You know I will," Faith hissed.

"There are two kids in the barn," I blurted, just in case something happened to me. The knife bit in deeper.

"Kids in the barn? Why?"

"Explain later," I choked out. The pressure against my windpipe increased.

How were we going to get out of this impasse?

The same question must have occurred to Jennifer. "This needs to end," she said, her voice softer. "Just put down the knife, Faith. We can talk about it, figure something out. Nobody needs to know about this."

Faith didn't respond. Was she thinking about it? Faith was pressed against me, her legs akimbo, panting. I could smell the tea on her breath, and her powdery perfume, and a little whiff of sweat and fear.

"You can get in your car and drive away and forget all about this," Jennifer said. "You haven't done anything wrong here. Not yet. And even if you did do something before, there isn't any proof. You can just walk away."

"What about the kids in the barn?"

"We'll get them out and take them home," she said soothingly, as if she were talking to one of her toddlers. "And then you can go home and go back to business as usual."

I felt the knife relax a little. Was it working? "Business as usual," she said. "That would be nice." Then she tensed again. "It's not going to happen, though. This one won't let it."

"I will," I protested.

"You went after me with a knife!"

"I was just trying to get you to put the gun down," I said. "I was afraid you were going to shoot me."

"I wasn't," she said. "I promise, I wasn't."

"I'm sorry. I didn't know that," I said. "Can we call a truce?"

There was another cold breeze, this time coming from the opposite direction from the door. Again, that sharp herbal scent of lavender.

At the same moment, the door slammed shut and the wind chimes in the corner started to jangle.

"What the..."

The pressure left my neck for an instant. I launched myself to the left and rolled away from Faith. When I came up, Faith was sitting in the middle of the room, legs still akimbo, one pink pump adrift on the worn carpet, the knife in her slack hand, as Jennifer leveled a shotgun at her head.

"Lucy," Jennifer said calmly, holding out her cell phone. "Would you be so kind as to call the authorities?"

"With pleasure," I said, scrambling to my feet and giving Faith a wide berth as I took Jennifer's phone and dialed 911.

∾

MOLLY AND EDWARD arrived at the same time, both frantic to see Ethan and June. Deputy Shames was in the living room, with Faith in handcuffs; I had rescued the two teenagers, who had been trying to bash their way out of the back of the barn with an old shovel. They were both in Dottie's kitchen now, drinking hot chocolate and looking both embarrassed and relieved.

Molly, still pale, burst out with "What were you thinking?" then immediately threw her arms around Ethan, holding him tight. "I'm so glad you're okay... but I still want to kill you!"

Edward, likewise, pulled his daughter June into a fierce hug. "Thank God you're okay," he murmured, then, after a long embrace, held her at arm's length and looked at her. "We're going to have to have a talk, though."

"As are we," Molly said, eyeing Ethan. "In fact, I think all four of us should discuss this together."

"Don't tell Dad!" Ethan blurted out.

Molly bit her lip and looked at me. I knew Alfie had been talking about sending Ethan to military school. This could be another big point in his favor. Molly turned to her son. "Dad and I are going to have to talk about this, but we want to hear what's going on with you. Why the vandalism?"

"It was my idea, Mrs. Kramer," June volunteered, chin out. "I wanted to do something meaningful. I talked him into it."

"Even if that's true," Molly said, "no one was holding a gun to his head." She paused. "Until today, anyway." At the thought, she pulled Ethan into a hug again.

When she released him, Ethan pushed a lock of floppy brown hair behind his ear and took a deep breath. "Mom... I know I'm in big trouble, and this probably isn't the best time to bring it up, but... I don't think I'm cut out for a normal job." He took another deep breath, then announced, "I want to be an artist."

Molly was quiet for a moment, absorbing the new information, then gave a short nod. "That's fine," she told him, and Ethan sagged in relief. "And I'm happy to support you in pursuing that, as long as you're not using other people's property as your canvases. But in the meantime, you've got some apologizing to do... and going forward, you're going to have to hold up your end of the bargain."

He slumped. "Apologizing?"

"And a lot more than that, to be honest. As for art? We'll talk about it more, but you can't cut out Dad and me. You have to talk to us, tell us what's going on."

"Dad'll kill me."

"Dad loves you. And we'll figure it out," Molly reassured him. Then she turned to June with a smile. "Nice to finally meet you, despite the circumstances. I don't approve of vandalism, but I'm glad at least the two of you were trying to work for good."

"You're not mad?" she asked.

"Oh, I'm mad," Molly said. "Don't get me wrong. But we'll all talk about it and figure out what the consequences will be and move on."

"I'm thinking repainting some barns would be a start," Edward said.

"Repainting barns? But the people who own them are horrible to animals!" June protested.

"Vandalism is still a crime," Edward said firmly. "I'm just hoping you won't be prosecuted."

Both teenagers paled. "What?" June said.

"There are ways to raise awareness," Edward said. "We can talk about them. But you can't destroy other people's property."

"But enough about that for now," Molly said. "Why the heck did Faith lock you two up in a smokehouse?" She sniffed. "You still smell like sausage."

June was the one to answer. She looked very young and small in her loose jeans and oversized PETA T-shirt. She was twisting a strand of hair nervously between two fingers. "We were scoping out the Smolak ranch—he sends his cattle to a feedlot—and we overheard her talking to some woman about paying someone to sign some paperwork so they could get access to a property?" She looked puzzled.

"The racket they're running with Sunset Home," I said. "They get a doctor to sign a form saying that older folks are incompetent, then send in a 'guardian' to deposit them in the home and take over all the finances. Then they cash out the property. The family has no say once the guardianship is set up; they're powerless."

"That's horrible!" June said.

"It is," I said.

Jennifer, who had been sitting at the end of the table hugging herself, looked up at me. "Did Faith Zapalac really kill my brother?"

"She did," I said.

"Why?"

"Let's go take a walk," I suggested. I didn't want to tell her everything I knew in front of the kids.

Leaving the two parents with their kids, we stepped out of the kitchen door into Dottie's backyard. The barn doors were open, with Faith's Escalade parked inside; I was so grateful that the kids were okay.

And that I was still alive.

"Let's walk down the path to the creek," I suggested, and we wound through the pasture, past the restored patch of grassland that Dottie had spent so many years nursing. A cool breeze came up from the creek, and I found myself thinking of poor Eva, and how her desire to do good had backfired.

"I still can't believe my brother's gone," she said dully.

"We never got along, but I still loved him. I just..." She stopped talking and a sob escaped her.

"I'm sorry," I said, reaching out and putting an arm around her shoulders.

"Thanks," she said, swiping at her eyes and taking a deep breath. "I'm afraid to ask, but I guess I need to know. What happened?" Jennifer asked.

"Eva was going to whistle-blow on a scheme between the nursing home, a doctor, and Faith to take over the assets of elderly folks," I said. "Faith killed her before she could tell the police what was going on."

"But what about my brother?" she asked.

"Apparently he figured out Faith had done in Eva and tried to blackmail her. So she lured him down to the wool shop and killed him, figuring she'd frame Edward; after all, Edward made no secret of the fact that he thought your brother killed Eva, at least with me."

"So my brother would take the fall for Eva and Edward would go to jail for murdering Jessie," she said. "And in the meantime, Faith gets to continue her money-making scheme untouched."

"Exactly," I said.

"And she was going to kill the kids, too. And you."

"Thank goodness you showed up when you did," I said. "What made you decide to stop by?"

"After I dropped the kids off at daycare, I decided to come up and visit Mom—she's not doing so hot at the moment. I was about to drive home when I had an urge to come by and check on things. I just... had a feeling."

I thought of the whiff of lavender, and the fallen mirror, and the jangling wind chimes. I'd felt my grandmother at Dewberry Farm before, but never anywhere else. Had she called the person she'd mentioned in my dream, Liesl, too? I sent a brief prayer of thanks to her, grateful to have her as a guardian angel of sorts.

"This sounds like a ridiculous time to be asking this question," she said, "considering everything that's gone on, but do you think this might help in stopping the sale of the house?"

"I should hope so," I said. "Is your mom thinking of moving back home?"

"I was kind of thinking I might float the idea of the kids and me moving in with her," she said. "I'd like them to know their grandma, and I want my mom to be able to stay in her home as long as possible. I'm going to see if I can do some freelance writing from home, and maybe get a little bit of outside help for when I'm not at home."

"That would be terrific," I said. "Although I know you and your mother haven't always gotten along."

"We're working on it," she said. "And I'd like my kids to be able to grow up in a small town, like I did, with family. Now that their dad and I aren't together... well, family is more important than ever."

"I get that," I said. "I think it sounds like a terrific idea. I hope you can work it out."

"Me too," she said. "It's going to be weird being here without Jessie, though. We had our differences... but he was still my brother."

"I know," I said, and pulled her into a big hug.

∽

ONCE THE POLICE were through and everyone was gone, I walked into Dottie's living room, looking at the scattered photographs and the upended mirror on the floor. Had it been my grandmother who had caused the ruckus?

Several of the photos had come loose from their frames. I carefully picked up the backings, and slowly reassembled them. I recognized a younger Dottie, with her two kids, along with several people I didn't recognize, wearing stiff, starched-looking clothes and severe expressions. There was a slightly blurry picture of what looked like Dottie as a girl, tucked in next to a smiling older woman in an apron; her grandmother? I wondered.

There were a few earlier ones, too, in black-and-white, that looked like they were from the '30s. One in particular drew my eye; it was a young woman with a look of sadness to her, despite the neat, collared dress and the hands folded in her lap. As I picked it up, something fell out of the back of the photo: a smaller black-and-white photograph of a baby swaddled in a blanket, face scrunched up, obviously newborn. Something else fluttered to the floor, too... a scrap of fabric.

When I picked it up, a jolt of recognition shot through me. The fabric was a small, square piece of felt in mustard and gray. I peered at the photo; unless I was mistaken, it was the same blanket Quinn had found in the box in her closet.

I pulled my phone from my pocket and dialed Quinn.

"Are you okay?" she asked. "I heard you were in trouble... I've been calling and calling!"

"I must have had my ringer off," I said. "I'm at Dottie's... I found something you might be interested in. Will you come?"

"Is everything all right?"

"Yes. It is now, anyway," I said. "But bring your fabric."

"What? The one from the box? Why?"

"I'll explain when you get here," I said, and hung up a moment later.

∽

"WHAT'S GOING ON?" Quinn asked when I let her into the front door of Dottie's house fifteen minutes later.

"All kinds of excitement," I said, giving her a quick rundown of the day. "But this is what I wanted to show you. Do you have the blanket?"

"Right here," she said, digging in her handbag and pulling it out.

"I think I found your missing piece."

Quinn blinked at me. "What?"

"Look," I said. "The mirror fell off the wall, and all these photos scattered on the floor. I was putting this one back together, and this baby picture and a scrap of fabric fell out." I handed her the photo of the young woman, with the smaller picture of the infant and the scrap of fabric on top of the frame.

"I don't understand," Quinn said, staring at the tiny blanket square. "How did it end up here?"

"I don't know," I said. "Is it a match?"

She picked up the square and held it up to the missing corner. "It is," she breathed.

"Look at the photo of the baby," I said.

Quinn peered at it. "It's the blanket," she breathed. She looked at me. "What does this mean?"

"I'm hoping Dottie will be able to help us," I said. "But I'm wondering if you and Dottie might not be related."

"You mean... maybe my grandmother was one of her relatives?"

"It was the thirties," I said. "Maybe someone got pregnant who wasn't supposed to."

"So they gave my grandmother up for adoption," Quinn

said, gazing at the photo of the sad woman. "This could be my great-grandmother, then."

"It could be," I said.

"I might see a slight resemblance in the eyes," she said. "But I might be grasping at straws."

I looked at the photo. "You might be right," I said, then pointed to a ringlet escaping from her neat hairstyle. "Looks like she might have had naturally curly hair, too."

Quinn touched one of her corkscrew curls. "Wouldn't that be something, to discover that I'm part of the Kreische family, after knowing them all these years?"

"Let's go see Dottie and talk to her," I said.

"Now?"

I shrugged. "Why not?"

"Okay," she said. "But you're driving. I'm not sure I trust myself right now."

As we stepped through the front door, I glanced back at the mirror I had righted on the mantel. Who had made it fall? I wondered. My guess had been my grandmother... but what if it was Liesl, the woman my grandmother had talked about in my dream?

And who was the woman in the photograph?

23

Dottie was staring out the window when we got to her room in Sunset Home a half hour later. We'd walked right past the front desk, not paying any attention to the protests of the young woman, and headed down the hall to see my neighbor.

"Dottie," I said. "Are you doing okay?"

"A little better," she said, her face wan. "It's just... it's hard to lose a child. A mother should never have to bury her child."

"No," I agreed, reaching for her hand. "It's the wrong order of things. I'm so sorry you're suffering."

She squeezed my hand and gave me a haunted look, then glanced over at Quinn. "This is your friend from the cafe, isn't it?"

"It is," Quinn confirmed, and reminded her of her name.

"Quinn. I remember now," Dottie said with a small smile.

I squeezed her hand again. "Did the police come by?"

"They did," she said, and the smile faded. "I can't believe it."

"I know," I said. Faith had finally confessed to Deputy

Shames that she'd cracked Jessie over the head with a rock before drowning him in the dye. I'd also found out who had vandalized my chicken coop and put up the scarecrow; it had been Jessie, trying to keep me from poking around in his business. I filled in the rest of the details for Dottie, but skimped on the details regarding the manner of Jessie's death.

"She was going to kill those children, too?" Dottie breathed. "That's monstrous!"

"I know," I said, and took a deep breath. "I have an odd question... have you ever noticed anything unusual around your house? Things moving unexpectedly?"

"You mean a ghost," Dottie said flatly.

"I guess so."

She nodded. "We don't like to talk about it, but there's always been one."

"We found this in one of the photos that tumbled to the floor when the mirror fell," I said, and showed her the scrap of fabric and the baby picture.

"You think our ghost dropped the mirror?"

"I'm thinking it's possible," I said. "I'm also wondering if maybe your ghost wanted us to find this."

"What is it?" she asked, peering at it. "I've never seen this before in my life."

"It was behind this photo," I said, showing it to her.

"That was my grandmother, Elisabeth Kreische," she said. "She's the one who taught me all about plants, and how to use them to make dyes. We had a wonderful relationship. I miss her."

"This may seem like an odd question," I said, "but do you know if she had a child she put up for adoption? Around the mid-thirties?"

Dottie shook her head. "Not that we ever heard," she

said. Then her face got still. "Wait. There was a family story that she got sick and had to go to Houston for treatments for almost a year. When she got back, she wasn't quite the same for a while. That would have been about the right time period." She looked up at me. "You don't think... did she go because she was pregnant and had to have the baby out of town?"

Quinn and I exchanged glances. "The timing lines up," Quinn said.

"So she took a picture of her little one and kept it, along with a piece of the baby blanket she made for it. For your grandmother," Dottie said, looking at Quinn and reaching for her hand. "That would mean we're kin."

Quinn's eyes teared up. "I just did a DNA test, and it turns out I'm part German.

"Elisabeth was German," she said. "Her nickname was Liesl."

"What?" I said, feeling the hairs rise on my arms.

"Liesl," Dottie repeated. "Why?"

"I... I had a dream," I said. "It sounds ridiculous, but my grandmother was in it. She and I were baking, and someone came to the door. She brought me a big basket, like a bassinet, with a needle and some dyed wool yarn in it, and told me I was supposed to patch things up."

"We've had a basket bassinet in the family for ages," Dottie said. "When we get home, I'll show it to you." Then her face fell. "If I get home."

"I'm working on it," I said. "I can't imagine the sale will go through now that all of this has come to light."

"You think?"

"I'll do everything I can," I said.

"Liesl," Quinn said quietly, staring at the photo of the sad young woman. "She wanted me to know who my family was."

"It sure looks like it," I said. "I can't wait to see what happens when you put your name into Ancestry.com.

"That may be the only way I find out for sure," she said.

"And maybe you'll even find out who your grandfather was," I said.

"We're putting the cart before the horse, though," Quinn said. "We don't know for sure, do we?"

"Her eyes look like yours," Dottie said. "And she had corkscrew curls. You can't see it in this picture, of course, but it was red and curly. Just like yours."

At that, Quinn burst into tears. Dottie held out her arms, and the two hugged for a long, long time while I wiped a tear away from my own eye.

There had been a lot of losses in Buttercup lately. It was so nice to see something precious found.

∼

I'D JUST PULLED into my own driveway when my phone buzzed. It was Tobias.

"I've got good news," he said.

"So do I," I told him. "Sort of, anyway. But yours first."

"I think I found Cinnamon!"

"What? Where?"

"I went out on a visit this morning to an older couple out near Giddings. They found her after the storm, wobbling around next to their driveway, and they took her in."

"How did she get there? Is she okay?"

"I don't know... maybe the storm picked her up and she got lucky. Anyway, she's better than okay," he said. "She's moved into their house. She's got a bed in the kitchen, they bottle-feed her at regular increments, and they've named her Baerli."

"Barely? As in, almost not enough?"

He laughed. "No... it was one of the goat names in *Heidi*. It means 'little bear.'"

"That makes a lot more sense."

"The only thing is, they're pretty attached to her. It's going to be tough for them to give her up."

I understood that.

"How is the new addition getting along, by the way?" he asked.

"You know, with all the excitement, I haven't checked."

"Excitement?"

As I warmed up a bottle of milk to feed the new addition, I filled him in on everything that had happened.

"I can't believe it," he said. "Faith kidnapped Ethan and June?"

"She did. I hate to think what would have happened if we hadn't found out what they were up to and managed to figure out where they might be," I told him, shivering. "Molly and Edward aren't thrilled with their recent activities, but I think now that everything's out in the open, maybe there's some room to turn things around."

"I just hope they don't end up paying too much in damages," he said. "Ed Zapp lost a lot of chickens... I'm not sure how many he's gotten back. And painting barns can be expensive."

"Summer's coming," I said. "And Ethan was interested in art; maybe he can practice with a paintbrush and several cans of latex paint."

Tobias laughed. "That's one way to look at it. Still, though... I can't believe Faith would do something like that."

"I know."

"Come to think of it, though, when I was at Rosita's the other day, I overheard her talking about an agency from La Grange that was undercutting her commissions and taking some of her business," he said.

"So some of her revenue stream was drying up, and this deal was her new retirement plan."

Tobias sighed. "I know she's been involved in some shady deals before, but I never thought she'd start killing people to protect her profits."

"Or committing additional murders to avoid going to jail."

"Although that seems to have backfired. Poor Eva," he said. "And Jessie, too. I didn't much like him, but he didn't deserve to die."

"I feel the same way. I talked with Jennifer; she's going to see if she and her kids can move in and take care of Dottie."

"Really? That would be great!"

"I'm so glad she'll still be next door," I said as I filled a bottle with warmed goat milk and screwed the nipple on.

"Maybe you could talk to them about leasing some land," he said. "That would give them less to take care of and a little extra income. Your growing flock could use some more room."

"That might be helpful," I said, stepping out the back door and looking out at the green swathe of pasture next door. "Maybe not to plant crops, but if she'd be willing to let me use some of her pasture... that's a great idea!"

"Let me know how it works out," he said as I walked down to the barn. "How's the kid doing?"

"I'm just about to check," I said. A moment later, I opened the barn door and walked over to the stall where I'd left the three goats to get acquainted, fully expecting to see the new arrival huddling in the corner.

Instead, I saw Carrot munching hay while Niblet and Thistle, standing shoulder to shoulder, were—almost—peacefully nursing. "You're not going to believe this," I said, "but it worked!"

"They're getting along?"

"Both kids are nursing, and Carrot's snacking on hay," I said.

"That's terrific!" he said. "I wasn't sure it would work... that's great news. The only issue is... what do you want to do about Cinnamon? Or Baerli, as the case may be."

I watched the three goats as I considered the best solution. "She seems pretty happy where she is?"

"She does," he said. "And the Argyles are over the moon with her."

"They should stay together then," I decided. "And if she becomes too much, she's welcome here."

"I'll let them know," he told me. "I think it's a good call. Three kids might be a lot for Carrot, and I don't want to do anything that might upset the truce with the newcomer. Unless you'd like to go back to bottle-feeding every few hours for the next several weeks..."

"No thank you," I said. "I think the current arrangement will work out just fine."

"I'll let them know, then," he said.

Less than two hours before, I reflected as I watched my new goat family, I'd been trapped in a barn with two teenagers and a murderer. Now, my main concern was whether my new broccoli starts were looking a little dry.

It wasn't a bad way to end an afternoon.

24

The Saturday before Easter Sunday was the last day of the Easter Market. The morning dawned bright and clear, with a cool breeze from the north. We'd had a gentle rain shower the night before, and the veggie starts were all happy, their little green leaves plump and glistening in the morning light.

I finished my chores early, and even though mucking out stalls wasn't my favorite task, I was grateful to see that Niblet was thriving with Carrot and Thistle. The hens had finally started laying, and I was delighted to have several cartons to take to the market. As I gathered the last of the herb starts and loaded them into the truck next to the cooler of cheese and eggs, something was niggling at me, but I couldn't think what it was. It wasn't until I'd smoothed out the bright white tablecloth, set out the last of the dyeing packets and glanced across the market to Gus's birdhouse stall that I figured out what it was.

I still didn't know why Gus Holz had been having dinner with Eva in La Grange.

There was still fifteen minutes before the market officially opened, so I took the opportunity to stroll across the town green to where Gus was busy hanging a hot-pink birdhouse from a hook.

"Hey," I said. "How's it going?"

"I've sold about a dozen so far this market," he said. "I was worried at first, but the colored houses have really started to take off. Flora's started painting some of them, too," he said, pointing to a pretty little church-style house with bushes painted around the perimeter, bright songbirds nestled in the foliage.

"You two seem superhappy," I said.

"We are," he admitted, his weathered face splitting into a grin. "I always thought I'd spend the rest of my years alone. Now that I've got Flora, though, it's all different. Even if she does want to put lace curtains in my kitchen."

I was glad to see him light up when he talked about Flora; after all, I was the one who encouraged her to date him. But there was that one niggling thing. "I have something of an awkward question to ask," I said.

"Shoot," he said.

"How did you know Eva Clarke?"

His face fell a bit. "Poor Eva," he said. "It's a shame what happened to her. Heard it was Faith Zapalac who did her in."

"Seems that way," I said. "Someone mentioned seeing you two at dinner in La Grange not too long ago."

His eyes widened in horror. "Oh, no. Is there a rumor going around town that I was steppin' out on Flora?"

"There was some talk that that might be the case," I admitted. "I just wanted to check in. Flora's my friend."

"That wasn't it at all!" he said. "Eva knew my old mentor had been moved to that Sunset Home place. She thought there was something funny about how his estate had been handled, and wanted to ask me what I knew about it. She told me not to tell anyone about it, though... that's why we met in La Grange, not Buttercup."

"So it was about Sunset Home?'

"She was thinking of callin' the police on 'em," he said, "but wanted to get her ducks in a row first." He sighed. "Looks like she was on the right track."

"She was, it seems," I said, relieved that there was a good explanation for the mystery dinner. As he spoke, I caught a whiff of rose perfume. Gus's face lit up.

"There's my girl," he said as Flora bustled up to his stall, looking a little like an Easter egg in a bright yellow skirt with purple stripes and a poofy purple blouse. She'd really come into her own, and her new relationship had made her blossom; it warmed my heart to see it. Gus gave her a quick kiss, which she returned happily. She was radiant.

"Lucy!" she said, turning to me. "I heard you had some excitement this week!"

"Too much," I said.

"Thank goodness Molly's boy and his friend are okay. It's a shame about Eva and Jessie, but at least you found the murderer. They should make you sheriff instead of that ol' Rooster, I swear!"

"Thanks, but I think I'm happier farming," I said. "If I could just find some way to make the weather more predictable, it would be perfect."

"I heard about your crops," she said. "I'm so sorry. If you ever need a little extra acreage, let me know," she said. "I know it's a drive, but I'd be happy to work something out with you. Mama's land is a lot to manage."

"You're sweet," I said. "I'm thinking of asking Dottie if I can lease some of her land, since it's right next door, but may I keep your offer in mind?"

"Of course. I still owe you," she said. "After all, without you, I might not be here... and Gus and I might not be together!" She gave him another peck on the cheek, and he blushed. "We keep meaning to invite you and Tobias over to dinner. I've got plans for Gus's kitchen, and we need your input."

"I'd love that, and I know Tobias would, too," I said. "Just tell us when to show up and what to bring!"

"Maybe some of your wonderful goat cheese?" she asked. "I'm going to pick some up today, anyway. By the way, I saw the ad in the *Zephyr*. Did you ever find your lost kid?"

"I did," I said. "She's cozily ensconced with a retired couple who have renamed her and given her the run of the place."

"Are they going to be okay giving her up?" Flora asked, a furrow appearing between her brows.

"I've decided to let them keep her," I said. "We found another orphaned kid and she seems to be getting along great, so we're going to let things be."

"That's so nice of you!" she said. "Thank goodness that little one made it. I was worried."

"Me too," I said. "But all's well that ends well."

"Except for Eva," she pointed out.

"And Jessie," I said, and my heart ached. How was Dottie doing? I wondered. I glanced at my watch. "I'd better get back before things pick up," I said.

"Let's plan dinner this weekend!" Flora said.

"That would be great," I said, smiling as Gus gave her a kiss on the top of the head. At least one thing was going right.

I'd just put out some goat cheese samples when Jennifer appeared, pushing her mother in a wheelchair, with two small children hanging onto the armrests. "Jennifer! Dottie!

I'm so glad to see you!" I smiled at the little boy Liam, who was staring wide-eyed at the dyed eggs on the table. "And your kids are adorable!"

"Thanks," Jennifer said, her eyes crinkling into a smile. "Liam? Kayla? This is Miss Resnick." Kayla extended a chubby, sticky hand, and I took it solemnly. "She's going to be our new neighbor!" Jennifer added.

I looked up. "You're moving to Buttercup?"

"Mother and I talked about it. I hired an attorney... she says she should be able get us out of the contract. I'll move in and help Mother manage the place, and the kids will get to grow up in Buttercup, just like I did."

"That's wonderful," I said. "I'm so sorry about your son," I told Dottie, "but I'm glad you'll be moving back in."

"Thanks," Dottie said. "And thanks for finding out what happened to my boy," she said, tears coming to her eyes. "You've always been so good to me."

"Happy to help," I said, meaning it. "I'm just sorry it turned out the way it did, but I'm glad Jennifer and the kids will be moving back to live with you."

"Me too," she said, reaching up for her daughter's hand and squeezing it. "It's been a long time. We had some patching up to do."

Jennifer smiled, tears in her eyes. "We did," she said in a soft voice. "And we have some new family, too. The kids have a new cousin."

"Quinn," I said, smiling. "I'm so glad it's going well. I know she's absolutely thrilled."

"So are we," Jennifer said. "I'm just sad I didn't know earlier... but at least we found out now. By the way," she added. "Mother and I talked about your farm... Quinn mentioned you were looking for a little more space?"

"I might be," I said. "I could certainly use some more pasture for my growing herd."

"The farm's a bit big for me to handle these days," Dottie said. "I'd like to sell you some of my acreage, if you're interested."

"I am!" I said. "I'm a bit strapped right now is the thing, what with the renovations on the little house and the tornado hitting."

"Oh, don't worry about that," Dottie said, waving my concerns away. "We'll work something out. The important thing is that it's in the hands of someone who will take care of it. And I know you will."

"That would be wonderful," I said. "Oh—by the way, I keep meaning to give this to you." I dug in my purse and pulled out the locket I had found on the day of the tornado. "I found this right after the storm."

Dottie's eyes widened as I lowered it into her hand from the chain. "You found this during the storm? My grandmother lost this years ago," she said. "I never knew what was in it, but she always wore it."

"There's a lock of hair in it," I said.

Dottie's eyes softened. "Probably from the little girl she had to give up." She reached for her daughter's hand; Jennifer took it and squeezed. "She grieved for a week when it came up missing." Again, there was that chill in the air, and I felt goose bumps on my arms.

I think Dottie felt it, too. She raised her head, and there was... a listening expression of sorts on her face. "I wonder," she said.

"I think I've felt her," I said quietly. "I think she's looking out for you."

"Really?" Dottie said, smiling.

"For both of us, really," I said. *Have I done enough to patch things up?* I asked silently. There was no response, but then I didn't really expect one.

"Well," Dottie said, shaking herself as if to bring herself back to the present. "Thank you for this; I'll treasure it. And as soon as we get this contract off the books, let's talk." She looked at me and dabbed at the corner of her eye. "And thank you again. For everything. You're the best kind of neighbor."

"So are you," I said, feeling my heart swell. Buttercup was a beautiful place, but the best thing about it was the people.

~

It was a good day at the Market. I'd sold almost everything, and even had orders for goat cheese and more herb starts. Molly had invited Edward, June, Tobias and me to dinner as a thank you for finding the kids... and as an olive branch to Edward, I suspected. Tobias came over after the Market, and we spent the afternoon making my favorite pecan pie recipe. Chuck followed my every step around the kitchen, snapping up a few crumbs of dough that fell to the floor as I trimmed the edges of the pie pan.

"It was an accident," I said to Tobias, who was measuring out pecans for the filling. My grandmother's cookbook was on the counter; just reading her spidery writing made me feel like she was in the kitchen with me. As if in response, I caught the sharp scent of lavender.

"Do you smell that?" I asked Tobias.

"Smell what?"

"Lavender," I said.

He took a sniff. "All I smell is pie dough."

"Maybe it's just me," I said, although I knew it wasn't. My grandmother was here. "Thank you," I whispered as Tobias walked to the pantry to retrieve the sugar canister. I was sure she was the one who had helped save us from Faith. The scent intensified for a moment, then faded. I touched the page with my grandmother's writing, filled with love and gratitude. I smiled and then gently pressed the dough I'd just made into the pie pan, trimming the edges. A piece fell on the floor just as Tobias returned with the canister.

"No wonder the diet isn't working," he commented as Chuck snapped up the bit of dough. "Just don't give him any pecans. They're not good for dogs."

I grinned. "The pie scraps were an accident. I swear!"

"Uh-huh," the handsome vet said, his eyes twinkling.

I looked at Tobias, and Chuck, and the beautiful rolling landscape out the slightly wavy glass of the kitchen window, and breathed another thank-you. Life in Buttercup might have its speed bumps and sadnesses, but it was a rich life, filled with people I loved, and I was beyond grateful.

~

EDWARD'S TRUCK was parked in the driveway when we pulled up at Molly's house just after six. I heard laughter inside as I rang the doorbell, and the Kramers' dog, Barkley, let out a large woof as Molly answered the door. My friend looked happier than I'd seen her in weeks.

"Come on in!" she said.

"We brought pecan pie," I told her, proffering one of the two pies that had come out of the oven an hour earlier. Tobias held the other.

"My favorite," she said. "With homemade crust, too, it looks like!"

I smiled as I followed her and Barkley into the kitchen. "Of course."

"It'll be perfect after Alfie's pork ribs," she said. "I made my grandma's potato salad. And then we're going to have the kids dye eggs with some of your dyeing packets."

"That sounds fabulous... but pork ribs and potato salad?" I said. "Had I known, I would have put on drawstring pants."

"Me too," Edward said. He was sitting next to Alfie at the kitchen table; both were drinking Shiner Bock longnecks, and both were smiling. They stood up as Molly and I entered.

"Thanks so much for getting our Ethan out of a sticky situation," Alfie said, walking around the table and pulling me into a big, barbecue-scented hug. Molly's husband was the size of a linebacker, but kind and firm. He always made me feel doll-size—which was saying something, because I wasn't a particularly small person. He let me go and smiled, the weathered skin around his eyes crinkling. "If you hadn't shown up when you did, I hate to think what might have happened."

Edward gave me a hug, too; unlike Alfie, he smelled of paint thinner and aftershave. "I can't tell you how thankful we are."

"I'm as relieved as you are," I said. "We got lucky."

"Mandy Vargas sure got herself a scoop, didn't she?" Alfie said. "I heard the Houston Chronicle picked up the story."

"She did," I said. "Judge McLain and Dr. Frederick have been suspended and are under investigation; odds are good both of them will end up in jail."

"Not to mention Faith," Molly said. "She deserves it. I can't believe she was going to hurt those kids!"

"I know," I said.

"What about those poor people at the home?" Molly asked.

"Marcie Auckland has been calling on her network to

help the residents find representation and hopefully recover their rights... and at least some of their assets. I'm not sure if they're closing the home or if it'll be under new management."

"Where are the residents in the meantime?"

"The administrator has been fired," I said. "They've got a skeleton crew coming in to take care of things, and lots of oversight, but it's going to take a while to sort out."

"Sounds like it," Alfie said. "A bad business."

"It is," I said. "How are the kids doing?"

"June and Ethan? Doing okay, it seems. They're out in the barn," Molly said. "Now that it's all out, they've told us everything they were up to."

"Anything new?"

"They confessed to a bit of experimentin'," Alfie said. That explained the cigarettes and beer cans. "But mainly they were tryin' to raise awareness of ranchers and farmers who mistreat animals. I can't say I disagree with 'em, but they can't go around paintin' barns and lettin' folks' livestock run free."

"We talked to the farmers and ranchers," Molly said. "They'll be willing to let it ride as long as the kids come back and fix the damage."

"And write apologies," Alfie added.

"So no charges," I said.

"No charges," Molly said. "Thank goodness. And I need to tell those two dinner is about to start, come to think of it," she said.

"I'll go tell them," I said.

"Thanks. I'll round up the other kids," Molly said.

As Tobias popped the cap off a Shiner Bock and joined Alfie and Edward, I let myself out the back door and headed for the old red barn close to the house. Ethan and June were just inside the door, heads close together, deep in conversation.

"Hey," I said.

They jumped, and June let out a squeak.

"Sorry to scare you," I said.

"It's okay," June said, crossing her arms. "I think we're just still a little freaked out."

"I am too, frankly," I said. "It was pretty terrifying."

"Why would she do that?" June asked.

"Who knows? People do strange things," I said. "By the way, I hear you worked things out with your folks."

"Sort of," Ethan said, grimacing. "We have to meet here, now, at least for a while."

"And we have to apologize and paint over all the barns," June burst out. "These people are being horrible to animals! And we're supposed to make nice with them?" There were tears in her eyes.

"June, we've got to do it," Ethan said.

"I know," she said. "But it's so wrong. What about those poor animals?"

"I get it," I said. "I feel the same way; it doesn't seem fair, in some ways."

"It doesn't."

"But just because you have to repaint some barns, that doesn't mean you have to stop making your voices heard."

June crossed her arms. "How else are we supposed to protest?"

"Write letters to the editor," I said. "Start a Facebook group. Grow your organization... get other kids to join, and maybe they can influence their parents. Volunteer for PETA. Maybe learn about animal husbandry from someone like Peter, and then find some way to educate ranchers and farmers about different practices. Heck," I said. "Maybe you could set up some talks at the school's FFA. I'm sure Peter would be happy to come in and talk about his farming practices."

"Or you," June pointed out. "You take care of your livestock."

"I do," I said.

June bit her lip. "I heard about you losing a baby goat in the storm. Did you ever find her?"

"I did," I said.

"Is she okay? Is she back with her mother?"

"Actually, she's been adopted by a retired couple who named her for one of the goats in Heidi. She's got the run of the whole house. I told them they could keep her."

"They have a house goat?" June asked, her face lighting up. "That's hilarious."

"I know, right? At any rate," I said, "I'm supposed to call you in for supper. It's ribs."

"I'm vegetarian," June said.

"There's potato salad, too."

"With bacon in it," June pointed out.

"All right. There's pecan pie, then," I said.

"Pecan pie?" June asked. "My favorite!"

"I brought two, so there will be plenty. Let's go!"

The two teenagers followed me into the house, where everyone was already gathered. Alfie had put a huge platter of pink, smoky ribs on the table, Molly had added a giant bowl of potato salad, studded with parsley and glistening with oil, and the long table was filled with smiling faces. On the counter, two dozen boiled eggs waited to be colored, and one of Quinn's mazanec breads was on the breadboard next to the toaster.

"We may never have to eat again," Tobias said as we sat down at the crowded table.

"If only that were the case," I said as I reached for the bowl of potato salad and smiled as Edward got about half a cup of barbecue sauce stuck in his beard while everybody laughed. Despite the tragedies of the last week, I could feel the mending within Molly's family, and some new threads being formed between newcomers Edward and June and the Kramer clan.

I put down the potato salad spoon and reached for the ribs, feeling a wave of gratitude for the blessings of life in Buttercup.

"Don't forget to save room for pie," Tobias reminded me.

"There's always room for pie," I said as I helped myself to three or four of Alfie's ribs. As I surveyed my full plate and the laughing faces at the table, I felt a deep satisfaction well up inside me. I might not have the biggest bank account on the planet, and it might be a lean couple of months on Dewberry Farm as the crops recovered from the storm. But if family and friends were the measure, I was the wealthiest person I knew.

MORE BOOKS BY KAREN MACINERNEY

To download a free book and receive members-only outtakes, short stories, recipes, and updates, join Karen's Reader's Circle at www.karenmacinerney.com! You can also join her on Facebook at facebook.com/AuthorKarenMacInerney and facebook.com/karenmacinerney.

And don't forget to follow her on BookBub to get newsflashes on new releases and sales!

The Dewberry Farm Mysteries
Killer Jam
Fatal Frost
Deadly Brew
Mistletoe Murder
Dyeing Season
Wicked Harvest (Fall 2019)

The Gray Whale Inn Mysteries
Murder on the Rocks
Dead and Berried
Murder Most Maine

Berried to the Hilt
Brush With Death
Death Runs Adrift
Whale of a Crime
Claws for Alarm
Scone Cold Dead (Summer 2019)
Cookbook: The Gray Whale Inn Kitchen
Blueberry Blues (A Gray Whale Inn Short Story)
Pumpkin Pied (A Gray Whale Inn Short Story)
Iced Inn (A Gray Whale Inn Short Story)

The Margie Peterson Mysteries
Mother's Day Out
Mother Knows Best
Mother's Little Helper

Tales of an Urban Werewolf
Howling at the Moon
On the Prowl
Leader of the Pack

RECIPES

DEWBERRY FARM SHRIMP AND GOAT CHEESE QUESADILLAS

Quesadilla Filling

Ingredients:

1/2 pound medium shrimp, unpeeled
4 ounces goat cheese
1 cup grated Monterey Jack cheese
2 tablespoons cilantro, minced
1/2 teaspoon fresh garlic, minced
1/2 teaspoon salt
1/4 teaspoon black pepper

Fill a medium saucepan half full of water. Bring to a boil and add shrimp; stir once, and cook for three minutes. Drain and set aside until cool, then peel shrimp and chop coarsely. In a medium mixing bowl, combine goat cheese, Monterey Jack cheese, cilantro, garlic, salt, pepper and shrimp.

Verde Sauce

2 pounds fresh tomatillos
2 cups yellow onions, minced
1 teaspoon fresh garlic, minced
1/4 cup fresh cilantro, minced
1 teaspoon fresh jalapeño, seeded and minced
1 tablespoon fresh oregano, minced
Pinch of sugar
1/2 teaspoon salt
2 cups water

Place whole tomatillos in a sink full of hot water and allow to sit for 15 minutes while skins loosen. Remove skins. Put tomatillos and remaining ingredients in a large, heavy stock pot. Bring water to a boil. Lower heat. Simmer for 1 hour, stirring occasionally. Puree in small batches in a blender or food processor until smooth.

Assembly

1 recipe Quesadilla filling
8 flour tortillas
4 teaspoons butter, divided
1 cup Verde Sauce

Lay four flour tortillas out on a countertop and place one fourth of filling on each tortilla. Spread filling evenly over the entire tortilla and place one of the remaining tortillas on top of filling. Press firmly. Repeat with remaining tortillas and filling.

Dewberry Farm Shrimp and Goat Cheese Quesadillas

Melt one teaspoon butter in a medium non-stick pan over medium heat. Place one quesadilla in skillet and cook for 3 minutes on each side. Hold in a 200 degree oven until ready to serve. Repeat with remaining butter and quesadillas. Cut each quesadilla into quarters with a pizza cutter. Serve with salsa verde.

Note: Use extra verde sauce for enchiladas or as a dip for chips!

DEWBERRY MARGARITAS

Ingredients:

Dewberry or Blackberry Puree

2 pints fresh dewberries or blackberries
1/4 cup sugar
Juice of 1/2 lime

Lime Sugar

2 cups sugar
Zest of 3 limes
1 lime wedge

Margaritas

2 cups tequila
1/2 cup triple sec
1/2 cup sugar
2 limes

Ice

Directions:

For the puree: Add the berries to a medium saucepan with the sugar and lime juice. Cook over low heat, covered, 20 to 25 minutes. Strain using a fine mesh strainer, pressing the berries to extract as much juice/puree as possible. Place in the fridge to cool completely.

For the lime sugar: Mix together the sugar and lime zest. Use a piece of lime to moisten the rim of each margarita glass, and then dip in the lime sugar.

For the margaritas: In a blender, add 1 cup of the tequila, 1/4 cup of the triple sec, 1/4 cup of the sugar, and the juice of 1 lime. Fill the blender with ice and blend until smooth. Then add as much blackberry puree as desired, 1/3 to 1/2 cup.

Pour into 4 rimmed glasses and serve immediately. Repeat with the rest of the ingredients for the other 4 glasses.

QUINN'S BLUE ONION MAZANEC

Ingredients:

4 cups all-purpose flour
3/4 cup granulated sugar
1 package instant dry yeast
6 1/2 tbs unsalted butter, softened
1/2 tsp salt
1 tsp pure vanilla extract
10 fl oz lukewarm milk
1/4 cup raisins
1/4 cup sliced almonds
1 egg plus one egg yolk
1 tbs water

Directions:

Mix the package of yeast with the lukewarm milk in a small bowl. Add a pinch of sugar and stir gently, then cover with a kitchen towel and let stand until the mixture is frothy (about

5 minutes). While yeast is proving, soak raisins in boiling water until plump, then drain and set aside.

Cream together softened butter and sugar with an electric mixer. Add in egg yolk, salt and vanilla extract, then mix until mixture is smooth and creamy. Add yeast mixture and mix again. Add flour in three portions until completely combined. Add raisins and mix with the dough hook attachment for about a minute, until a soft dough forms. Place the dough in a large, greased bowl, cover with plastic wrap sprayed with cooking spray and let rise in a warm spot for at least an hour, or until it has doubled in size.

Once the dough has risen, remove from the bowl and shape it into a ball, smoothing out the surface. Place dough on a baking sheet lined with parchment paper and cover with a kitchen towel. While dough is rising, preheat oven to 350 and whisk an egg with about a tablespoon of water in a small bowl. When dough has risen (about a half hour), remove towel and brush loaf with the egg wash, then sprinkle generously with the sliced almonds. Bake for 45 – 55 minutes, until the loaf is golden brown and sounds hollow when tapped on bottom. If the loaf begins to brown too quickly, cover with foil to prevent it from burning.

Let cool, then slice and spread with butter and your favorite jam.

BUTTERCUP PECAN PIE

Ingredients:

3 eggs, beaten
3/4 cup sugar
3/4 cup white corn syrup
3 tbsp melted butter
1 tsp vanilla
1 tsp white vinegar
1/8 tsp salt
1 cup chopped pecans

Directions:

Mix all ingredients thoroughly, except the pecans. Add the pecans and pour in the mixture into an unbaked pie shell. Preheat oven to 375 and bake for 25-30 minutes. Testing for doneness with a knife inserted in the center. Pie is done when knife comes out clean.

Pie Crust (makes one two-crust or two one-crust pie shells)

Buttercup Pecan Pie

Ingredients:

2 cups flour
1 tsp salt
2/3 cup plus 2 tbsp shortening
4-5 tbsp ice-cold water

Directions:

In a medium size bowl, combine the flour and salt, then cut in shortening with a pastry blender or two forks. Sprinkle water 1 tbsp at a time until all flour is moistened, taking care not to overwork. Shape into a ball and roll out on floured surface.

GERMAN POTATO SALAD

Ingredients:

3 cups diced red, Yukon Gold, or new potatoes (peeling optional)
4 slices bacon
1 small onion, diced
1/4 cup apple cider or white vinegar
2 tablespoons water
3 tablespoons white sugar
1 teaspoon salt
1/8 teaspoon ground black pepper
1 tablespoon chopped fresh parsley

Directions:

Place the potatoes into a pot, and fill with enough water to cover. Bring to a boil, and cook for about 10 minutes, or until easily pierced with a fork. Drain, and set aside to cool.

Put the bacon in a cold skillet, then turn to medium-high

heat. Fry until browned and crisp, turning as needed. Remove bacon from the pan and set aside.

Add onion to the bacon grease, and cook over medium heat until browned. Add the vinegar, water, sugar, salt and pepper to the pan. Bring to a boil, then add the potatoes and parsley. Crumble in half of the bacon. Heat through, transfer to a serving dish, and crumble the remaining bacon over the top. Serve warm.

ALFIE'S SMOKED PORK RIBS

Ingredients:

6 pounds pork spareribs
1 1/2 cups white sugar
1/4 cup salt
2 1/2 tablespoons ground black pepper
3 tablespoons sweet paprika
1 teaspoon cayenne pepper, or to taste
2 tablespoons garlic powder
5 tablespoons pan drippings
1/2 cup chopped onion
4 cups ketchup
3 cups hot water
4 tablespoons brown sugar
cayenne pepper to taste
salt and pepper to taste
1 cup wood chips, soaked

Directions:

Clean the ribs, trimming away any excess fat. In a medium bowl, stir together the white sugar, 1/4 cup salt, ground black pepper, paprika, 1 teaspoon cayenne pepper, and garlic powder. Coat ribs liberally with spice mix and place the ribs in two 10x15 inch roasting pans lined with foil, piling two racks of ribs per pan. Cover and refrigerate for at least 8 hours.

Preheat oven to 275 degrees and bake uncovered for 3 to 4 hours, or until the ribs are tender and nearly fall apart.

Remove 5 tablespoons of drippings from the bottom of the roasting pans and place in a skillet over medium heat. Saute onion in pan drippings until lightly browned and tender. Stir in ketchup and heat for 3 to 4 more minutes, stirring constantly, then mix in water and brown sugar. Season to taste with cayenne pepper, salt, and pepper. Reduce heat to low, cover, and simmer for 1 hour, adding water as necessary to achieve desired thickness.

While sauce is cooking, preheat grill for medium-low heat.

When ribs are ready to grill, add soaked wood chips to the coals or to the smoker box of a gas grill (I put soaked chips in a "bowl" made of aluminum foil and place it on the burner beneath the grate). Lightly oil grill grate. Place ribs on the grill two racks at a time, making sure not to crowd them. Cook for 20 minutes, turning occasionally.

Baste ribs with sauce during the last 10 minutes of grilling to prevent sauce from burning.

NATURAL EASTER EGG DYES

Although Lucy used dried ingredients like turmeric for her dye packets, you can easily whip up natural dyes at home.

Red – Mix 2 cups of grated raw beets with 1 tablespoon of vinegar. Boil with 2 cups of water for about 15 minutes (other options include frozen cranberries and strong Red Zinger tea).

Yellow to Gold – Simmer 3 large handfuls of yellow/brown onion skins in 3 cups of water for about 15 minutes. Alternately, boil 2 or 3 tablespoons of ground turmeric or chamomile in 2 cups of water for about 15 minutes.

Blue – Boil 1 pound of crushed frozen blueberries in 2-3 cups of water for about 15 minutes. For lavender shades, use three cups of red cabbage leaves instead.

Notes:

Make the individual dyes in 3 different nonreactive

saucepans. For a uniform color, strain the dye mixtures through cheesecloth or a fine strainer. If you prefer mottled, or tie-dyed eggs, leave the ingredients in the pan with the cooked beets, onion skins, or blueberries, then put the eggs directly in the pan to soak with the cooked ingredients. (The longer you soak the eggs the deeper the color will be.) You can also experiment by combining the different dyes in coffee cups to get different colors. To make designs, use a white crayon prior to dyeing.

<<<<>>>>

ACKNOWLEDGMENTS

First, many thanks to my family, not just for putting up with me, but for continuing to come up with creative ways to kill people. (You should see the looks we get in restaurants.) I also want to give a shout-out to Carol and Dave Swartz and Bethann and Beau Eccles for their years of continued support.

Special thanks to the MacInerney Mystery Mavens (who help with all manner of things, from covers to concepts), particularly Gail Meredith, Marissa Lee, Mandy Young Kutz, Alicia Farage, Samantha Mann, Azanna Wishart, Priscilla Ormsby, Pat Tewalt, and Barb Wiesmann for their careful reading of the manuscript. What would I do without you???

Kim Killion, as usual, did an amazing job on the cover design, and Randy Ladenheim-Gil's sharp editorial eye helped keep me from embarrassing myself.

I want to give a big shout-out to the folks at Trianon Coffee-house for keeping me motivated (i.e. caffeinated) and being such terrific company. And finally, thank you to ALL of the wonderful readers who make Dewberry Farm possible, especially my fabulous Facebook community. You keep me going!

ABOUT THE AUTHOR

Karen is the housework-impaired, award-winning author of multiple mystery series, and her victims number well into the double digits. She lives in Austin, Texas with her sassy family and a menagerie of animals, including a rescue dog named Little Bit.

Feel free to visit Karen's web site at www.karenmacinerney.com, where you can download a free book and sign up to receive short stories, deleted scenes, recipes and other bonus material. You can also find her on Facebook at www.facebook.com/AuthorKarenMacInerney or www.facebook.com/karenmacinerney (she spends an inordinate amount of time there). You are more than welcome to friend her there—and remind her to get back to work on the next book!

P. S. Don't forget to follow Karen on BookBub to get newsflashes on new releases!

www.karenmacinerney.com
karen@karenmacinerney.com

Made in the USA
San Bernardino, CA
07 February 2020